MW00886531

Wicked Games

WICKED GAMES

Copyright © 2011 by Jill Myles

This story is a work of fiction. Names, characters, places, and incidents are either products of the author's imagination or used fictitiously. Any resemblance to actual events, locales, or persons, living or dead, is entirely coincidental.

All rights reserved.

No part of this publication can be reproduced or transmitted in any form or by any means, electronic or mechanical, without permission in writing from Jill Myles.

www.jillmyles.com

Wicked Games

JESSICA CLARE

MYLES | SIMS | CLARE

Chapter One

I'm looking forward to the competition. Test myself against elements...and the other players. Romance the ladies? If I need to. Anything to win, but I'm not specifically looking to meet a girl. I'm looking to win. —Pre-Game Interview with Dean Woodall

IN THE FOUR YEARS THAT I'D WORKED FOR *MEDIA WEEK* MAGAZINE, my boss had never seemed pleasant. I suspected she wasn't the smiley type unless she was signing your pink slip. Seeing that many white teeth in her mouth at once as I entered her office? I'd be lying if I didn't find it a little bit creepy.

"Hello Abigail," she cooed at me. "So very nice to see you again." She took me by the elbow and led me into the room, shutting the door behind her.

Another ominous sign. Well, that and my full name. All my friends called me Abby. My boss? She only called me Abby when...well, come to think of it, she'd never called me Abby.

I noticed another man was sitting in the room, a wide-brimmed adventurer's hat in his hands. He wore a shirt that looked like it had been yanked off of a safari tour and grinned at me, flashing more white teeth in my direction.

All these teeth. I was surely in trouble.

"Hi," I said lamely, not sure what else to say, and plunked down in the only open chair. My palms were sweating already, and I wiped them against my jeans. "What's going on?"

Jeannie trotted back around to her side of the desk, her heels clacking on the tile floor. She sat in her chair delicately and swung around to face me, clasping her hands in front of her and giving a sidelong glance to the stranger in the room. "Abigail, I've called you in because…we might have an interesting assignment for you. What's your current workload look like?"

Oh boy. If the boss had an 'interesting' assignment for me, I was totally doomed. I smiled through my pain and tried to sound busier than I really was. "I have a couple of editorial pieces I'm working on, and that two page spread for the fashion article next week—"

She waved her hands at me. "Oh. That stuff? Thank goodness. We can put you on something important, then. Mr. Matlock here will be working with you on this assignment."

The man in question looked over at me and peered, and I could have sworn he was checking out my legs. "She'd be good, I think. Seems to be in decent shape, young, and reasonably attractive."

"Reasonably? You sweet talker you," I said before thinking better of it. "I bet you tell that to all the ladies."

To my relief, he laughed it off. "And a personality. Even better."

Why the heck was my appearance some sort of criteria for the job? I did book reviews for an entertainment magazine, for heck's sake. I shot my boss a confused look. "What sort of assignment are we talking about?"

The man leaned forward and grinned again, as if sharing a secret. "I'm Jim Matlock."

Obviously I was supposed to know who he was. I racked my brain, thinking.

The look on his face grew vaguely insulted as moments passed and I remained blank. He glanced back at Jeannie, sitting back again.

"Jim Matlock," Jeannie stressed. "From *Endurance Island*. Executive producer."

"The game show?" I was surprised. "Really?" I'd caught a few episodes here and there of the first season—it had been all about pretty people on the beach, jumping through colorful hoops and eating bugs to win a big cash prize. Not really my thing, but I'd heard bits and pieces about it here and there. Mostly about how last year's finale had been a total letdown. Not that I could say that to him. "I hear you're about to start shooting season two," I said, deciding on tact.

"In the Cook Islands," he agreed, and the mega-watt smile returned. "I'm afraid the network is a little concerned about ratings, however, so we're resorting to a couple of different strategies in order to create a bit more buzz about the second season."

"Oh?" I said politely, wondering where this lead to me. "And you want me to give you a favorable review?" I guessed, though a few things didn't add up. The show was for the fall season and we were just hitting spring at the moment—far too early for a review. And a fake gushing review? Jeannie knew I hated those—I was known for my scathing book reviews and not my glowing ones. They didn't call me 'Abby the Book Bitch' for nothing.

"We want you to write, but not really for a review," Mr. Matlock began slowly.

Jeannie cut to the chase. "Jim has had a high profile player drop out at the last minute, and filming starts in three days. The parent company of his network—you know they own the magazine, darling—has decided to stick an insider into the show to give a 'first hand' exclusive experience to the thing."

"Can you run? Swim?" Matlock asked me.

My heart sank and my stomach gave a nervous flutter. "I don't really want to be on TV." God no. See my name mocked and reviled in the same magazine that I wrote in every week, mocking and reviling others? No thank you.

"There's a rather lucrative book deal attached to this after the show," Jeannie added in a sly voice. "With a guaranteed push at all major media outlets."

"And a TV special," Jim added.

A book deal? I swallowed hard at that. It would be a lot of money. A lot. And infamy. Money and infamy, always hand in hand. I glanced over at Jeannie, but her slender jaw was set in a firm manner that told me that if I refused, I wouldn't find myself with very many more assignments at *MediaWeek*, if ever again. Not that she could fire me if I refused…but she could conveniently edge me out the door over time.

Let's see—fame and fortune and six weeks of island misery and eating bugs? Or no fame, no fortune, and one severely pissed off boss?

I swallowed hard. "Why me out of the team? Why not Roger? Or Tim?" Both were handsome, young, athletic and gay. Tim was my best friend, and a media darling if there ever was one. Me, not so much. I tended to blend in with the wallpaper, and I preferred it that way.

"We need a female contestant," Matlock said without hesitation. "The one we lost was female, and we need the teams evenly balanced. Young and reasonably attractive helps as well."

That did narrow down the staff quite a bit. Old Mabel that did the crossword and Gertie that set the TV listings probably wouldn't be good picks. All the others I could think of had small children, so I was the only candidate. It really grated that they kept saying 'reasonably' though. Jeezus. Way to make me feel like their last resort. "Uh huh."

"Here's the deal, Abigail," Jeannie said in a blunt voice. "You go out there and join their little game show and don't tell anyone about the deal. You'll meet up with production assistants that will allow you to record a video diary every day, exclusive for MediaWeek's usage. You stay until you're voted out, and when you come back, you do the press tour like a good girl, write your articles that give us an exclusive inside look, and then you write your book. It gives *MediaWeek* a nice bit of leverage and free advertising, and Matlock's show gets a boost as well. That's how the parent company wants it. Do you understand?"

I understood. It kind of sounded like the entire thing had been decided long before I even went into the room. I glanced over at Matlock and found him studying my figure again, and I resisted the urge to wrap my arms around my torso and hide myself. "I'm uh…not a hundred percent familiar with the show. How long would I be out there?"

"Six weeks if you stay the entire time. Someone will be voted off every four days. The show starts with twenty-four people with fifteen elimination rounds total. After seven group eliminations, we'll go down to singles for the last ten and two will go to the final vote for the two million dollars."

Holy shit. Two million dollars on the line—I felt dizzy. "Can I win the millions?"

"Possibly. You'll have to be really good." He gave me a faint, smug smile.

Interesting. They were going to give me a shot at two million? Suddenly I was a lot more interested. "What if I'm the first one voted out?"

"You won't be," he said. Again, the patronizing smile. "Other than that, it will be played out as the game goes. If you are eliminated early, you can give everyone a behind the scenes look at the Loser Lodge."

A six week island get-away and a book deal any way I looked at it. I glanced over at Jeannie and she was giving me a death-glare. Islands or Boss From Hell. Coconut Hell or Editorial Hell. Sand in my swimsuit crack every day for two months, or Jeannie up my ass for the rest of my life.

I looked over at Matlock and gave him a game shrug. "Let's give it a shot, then."

"That's a girl," he crowed, and Jeannie smiled smugly.

Yeah, joy. Yay. Me on TV.

THE NEXT TWO DAYS WERE A WHIRLWIND, BUT THE MAGAZINE WAS there to help out. There were things to be covered for and trained on (my weekly articles), a cat to be boarded (dropped off at Tim's), utilities to be paid ahead of time (so I wasn't homeless when I returned), and an endless round of physicals and vaccinations for the actual show. Just when I needed a nap—or to run away screaming from all of it—I was shuffled onto a charter plane and flown out to Auckland, New Zealand. One of the assistants continually shoved objects into my hands as we rode on the plane. She asked me a million questions and continually handed me release forms and waivers. No piece of information was sacred—from the last time I'd had my period to my blood type to my swimsuit size to did I need a bikini wax before the show filmed?

I admit I freaked out a little over the bikini-wax thing. Exactly how much were they going to be showing on this gameshow? But I sucked it up and got waxed, because the alternative was worse.

It got worse as we progressed. Every time I made a concession, I had to give three more. While we were on the plane, the assistant sidelined me with something else. "And here's your bag of clothing for the next six weeks."

It looked really, really small. Unnerved, I picked it up and began to dig through it. The fabrics that touched my hand felt soft, lycra-ish. Swimsuits, I guessed, and a shirt or two. Nothing warm, nothing concealing. Too kind of them. "Great, thanks." My enthusiasm was evident in my voice.

"You need to change before we get on the plane," she chirped at me, beaming, and led me towards the nearest bathroom. "Strip off all of your old clothing and put on what's provided for you. We have corporate sponsors and you have to wear their logos."

Made sense, even if I wasn't crazy about it. But, yay bathroom. Of course, I discovered a few minutes later that the show was going to be a bit of a lesson in humility and identity.

The shirt I pulled out? Bright, vivid pink with my name—ABBY—emblazoned across both the front and the back in bold white letters. I suppose that was to help the audience figure out who we were easily. Lovely. With a grimace, I tossed the shirt aside and dug into the bag again. A string bikini—same pink. Same garish name across the backside of the panties. Yeah, well that wouldn't be getting much use, despite my new (and painful) hair-free bikini line. I tossed it aside as well.

At the bottom of the bag, there was one more bikini in a different style, and a swimsuit—a tankini. All in the same nasty pink with my name screaming across the chest. I also had a pair of water shoes and a pair of sneakers. That was it.

Six week's worth of beach clothing. They were kidding, right?

Chapter Two

Abby who? —Dean Woodall, Day 1

THE BLINDFOLDS DID AN EXCELLENT JOB—I HADN'T SEEN THE FACE of one single, solitary person. I could hear them and smell them around me, though. The faint scent of cologne, deodorant, and some girl's powdery floral perfume lingered in my nostrils as the plane descended, and we were shuffled out, blindfolds intact, and onto a boat. The motor purred as we were taken out onto the water, waves crashing against the sides of the boat. I sat with my small bag of clothes in my lap, my legs pressed against two other pairs of legs on either side of me.

Someone shuffled equipment near the front of the boat, and I heard the motor cut. The breeze ruffled my hair gently, a signal that we'd slowed down or stopped on the water. I heard the microphone flick on, and the crew talking to themselves in low voices.

"Are we ready?" called a familiar, overly-cadenced voice. I tried to place it, but couldn't without a face.

"Ready," intoned someone else. "In three…two…one…"

"Welcome," boomed the host, so loudly that I jumped slightly in my seat, my nerves on edge. "Welcome to Endurance Island! We are here in the famous Cook Islands, home to piracy and private, sandy beaches. This will be your home for the next six weeks, provided you can endure all the challenges that Endurance Island has in store for you! Who's ready to Endure?"

Silence met his question. Someone coughed.

"Cut, cut," the host yelled, annoyed. "You're supposed to respond when I speak to you. Enthusiastic! Jeezus."

One brave soul piped up, to my left. A woman. "I thought we weren't supposed to speak until we got to the Island."

"When I ask you something, you answer, understand me?" The man sounded unpleasant.

A rash of murmurs went through the boat, and after a momentary coaching, we tried it again. This time, when the host's voice trilled upward with 'Who's Ready To Endure?' we yelled and cheered like morons.

I *so* hoped the camera wasn't on my face at that moment, or it'd catch my look of disgust.

"I'm Chip Brubaker, star of Family TV's hit sitcom, *Too Full Of A House*!"

Aha. That was where I'd heard that annoying voice. The image of a too-skinny, storky blonde man crossed my mind, and I smiled wryly. I'd given Mr. Brubaker's horribly ghost-written memoir an F and he'd written me a nasty letter in response.

Sixty days of fun, coming right up. Yessirree.

"Your first challenge is about to start," Chip yelled in an overly cheerful voice.

Everyone tensed, sitting up.

"When I say 'Go', you'll take off your blindfolds and grab one of the luxury items off of the table in the center of the boat. You can only grab one item. From there, you will all swim out to shore—the first person to arrive on shore and ring the gong will win a special, additional prize. Are you all ready?"

Shit! No, I wasn't ready. I still had my sneakers on, and I was wearing too many layers—

"Take off your masks! Go! Endurance Island has begun!"

I ripped off my mask at the same time as everyone else, bodies flying into motion. Someone elbowed me in my face, and people shoved ahead, trying to get to the center of the boat where the table was laid out.

I was half a step behind everyone else. In my urge to catch up, I stumbled forward and tripped over someone's discarded mask, knocking into the press of bodies ahead of me.

The table pitched forward, spilling the contents on the ground, and the frenzy got worse, even as the other contestants cussed at me. "You stupid idiot!" some older guy yelled at me.

"Hey, fuck off!" I yelled back, then forgot I wasn't supposed to cuss on TV. Whoops. I shoved ahead with everyone else, and they shoved me back like a well-tanned mosh pit. Someone was stepping on my shoelaces and I pitched to the floor, my palms smacking against the bottom of the boat.

A heavy object pitched against my shoe. I reached down and grabbed it, not caring what it was at this point—a person on the far end of the ship had just splashed into the water and was swimming for shore. I shoved the heavy canister into my pack, threw it over my shoulders, and ran down the far end of the boat with the others.

I was the third one into the water, a man and a woman swimming ahead of me in frantic strokes. I adjusted my bag on my shoulders and dipped under the water, propelling myself forward.

Someone heavy landed on me, stepped on my shoulder, and shoved off.

I nearly took in a lungful of water at that, and clawed my way back to the surface, intending on giving a good yell at the asshole that had basically springboarded off of me. I saw a blur of blue, and then he was gone, moving through the water at an unholy pace, his movements steady and even and powerful. *Dark blue*, I thought to myself, wiping salt water out of my eyes as I took a deep breath. I'd remember that. Though I couldn't breast stroke, I managed to maintain a calm and easy pace as I began to swim for shore.

"Someone help me swim!" A girl shrieked in my ear, and the next thing I knew, she was clinging to my backpack. "Help me swim! I'm going to drown!"

No kidding, I wanted to shout in her ear. Her violent flailing was dragging me down with her. Still, I figured it wouldn't look good if I let some crazy bitch drown on day one, so I hooked her arms with mine and helped drag her to shore. It wasn't so far off, even if a flood of people were already surging onto the pale sands, Dark Blue leading the pack.

Oh well. I hadn't wanted that extra item anyhow.

A short time later, I dragged the flailing blonde girl into shallow-enough water so we could walk along the sandy ocean floor. I continued to help her forward, though a quick glance around showed that we'd fallen to the back of the pack.

As if sensing she didn't need me any longer, Blondie gave me a rough shove of disgust. "Get off of me, loser! I'm not helping you any longer!"

My mouth dropped, and when she splashed me, I got a lungful of salt water. Coughing, I wasn't able to protest that I'd been the one dragging her sorry butt to shore, something she'd neglected to point out to the two dozen people loitering on the beach, all staring at us.

That was my grand entrance to the game—dragging my weary, water-logged self onto the beach, dead last, coughing up a storm. Lovely.

One girl stumbled over, kicking sand into my face as I lay flat on the sand. "Ohmygawd," she shrilled in a high voice with a thick southern accent. "You guys, I think she's fixin' to need medical attention."

"I'm fine," I tried to protest between coughs, but I'd swallowed a good liter of salt water, and it was still determined to make its way back up my throat.

"She just swallowed a little water," said an arrogant male voice. "Let her suck it up. We're all here to play an athletic game—"

"I know," the Southern girl interrupted again. "But she's obviously not athletic. Did you see her thighs?"

I coughed and tugged my wet shirt down over my thighs. They weren't big thighs! They were just...normal girl thighs. Not the tanned, shapely twigs that Shanna (according to her bikini bottom) had.

"Maybe she deliberately gained weight for the show," a girl with a Boston accent piped in.

All eyes rotated back to me.

We hadn't been on the island for ten minutes yet, and I already wanted to hide in shame. I was still coughing, so I did the next best thing—shot them all the bird.

"She's fine," the one male voice said again, sarcastic.

I'd be willing to bet that the voice belonged to Dark Blue.

The others ignored me after that, most of them flocking to a tall, bronze Adonis nearby. He wore a shirt—dark blue—with the word DEAN sprawled across the damp chest, and was shaking hands with the other guys.

My nemesis.

"Good job," the others praised him, showering him with accolades as if he'd suddenly discovered world peace instead of landing in first place in a swim competition. Of course, he wore a smug, flashy white grin that told me he was used to getting compliments heaped on him.

I hated Dean on sight. Screw him.

I didn't care if he happened to be one of the hottest guys I'd ever seen, and that he pretty much hit all my kinks right up front. The usual guy I was attracted to was tall, muscular, tanned with dark hair and pale eyes. Dean fit the bill remarkably well, with a set of amazing cheekbones and a cocky grin that was quickly turning some of the other girls to jello.

He carried an axe in his hands, flipping it with casual ease—the obvious reward of this mini challenge. Camera crews were already on the beach, swarming in the distance as we milled around each other and made awkward introductions.

Everyone pretty much ignored me. I took those moments to take inventory of what I'd grabbed from the table. Digging through my soaking wet pack, I grasped the heavy canister that had felt like a bowling ball against my back as I swam.

Peanut butter. A very large, very heavy jar of chunky peanut butter. Absurdly pleased at that, I smiled and shoved it back into my bag. Food and protein. A nice secret weapon to have in my stash. I glanced over my shoulder furtively, and noticed Adonis had been paying attention to my bag rummaging. I scowled at him and shoved it back inside, ignoring the cocky smile on his face.

Hated him. Five minutes on the island and I already knew who I was voting for first.

Chip waded onto shore a brief time later, giving us his best Hollywood Dad smile and hamming it up for the cameras. He gestured to a long row of circles in the distance and had us stand on the colored disks. We randomly picked spots—pink disks for the female players and light blue disks for the male players. Once we were on each disk, sandy, wet and disheveled, the cameras zoomed in and Chip began to speak again.

"Now that you've all had a chance to get a good look at each other, it's time to pick teams."

A chorus of cheers arose from the assembled crowd. I clapped my hands slowly, waiting to hear what he had to say.

"We're going to do a school-yard pick. Who won the bonus prize?" Chip craned his neck and peered at us, as if it wasn't obvious that Adonis—sorry, Dean—had won it, judging from the fawning of the others. "Dean? Can you step forward please?"

The tanned god did so, casting a quick grin back at the rest of us, and moved to stand next to the host. Next to him, Chip put his arm around Dean's shoulders. "Dean, since you won the special prize, I want you to hand out the rest of these plaques to the team." As Dean did so, Chip continued speaking. "I want everyone to write their profession down on a plaque and hold it in front of their chest. The guys will get to pick their partners instead of the other way around."

"Partners?" Dean spoke up, and Chip gave him a subtle frown. I guessed that we weren't supposed to interrupt the host.

"Partners," Chip echoed, speaking louder and talking over Dean. "We're going to divide you into teams of two. One man, one woman."

What the heck was this, Seven Brides for Seven Brothers?

The others began to write on their boards with a piece of chalk, and I glanced down at mine. What to write? Journalist? Writer? God, could I sound any less athletic if I wrote down writer? After a moment's intro- spection, I decided upon 'Book Reviewer' and flipped my board around. I peeked down the line, wondering if my suspicions were correct.

The other plaques read, in order: Ex-Military, Actress, Swimsuit Model, Grad Student, Camp Counselor, Playmate, Stunt Double, and Medical Intern. One shorter woman had written 'Gymnast' and another had written 'Mareen Biologest'. Ten bucks said that she wasn't one—those big fake breasts would make it impossible for her to stay under the water.

My buddy that had insisted I drag her to shore, only to mock me once I'd saved her ass? 'Aspiring Model'.

The men drew numbers and arranged themselves on the sand with tribe flags depicting their team numbers. To my intense satisfaction, good ol' Dean had selected number 11 out of 12, something that obviously didn't sit too well with him. He had a sour expression on his face that delighted me.

The first guy picked—some dude with a chest full of tattoos and a ring in his nose. I guessed that he was going to pick the gymnast (male fantasy and athleticism all in one).

"I'll take the Playboy Bunny," he said, and broke into a smile.

The bunny—my other nemesis Shanna—giggled and bounced over to stand next to him in the sand. The ex-military woman—Ginger—made a noise of disbelief in her throat, and I had to concur. Who would have thought that the girl with big plastic hooters and a Southern accent would get picked over a gymnast and a stunt double in a survival competition?

The next guy picked—the 'Mareen Biologest'. This was turning into a rather laughable spectacle of a 'survival' show. Hotness seemed to be the key factor here.

The next two to be snatched up were the ones I suspected—Ginger the ex-military, Vera the gymnast, and Alys the stunt-double were the next to go, all to partners that looked as if they were relieved at the other choices. Soon enough, it was Dean's turn to pick, and no one was left but myself and Heidi at the far end of the line, still holding her Aspiring Model sign and giving everyone a sunny smile.

Oh crap.

I had a hunch that I'd be picked dead last—and the guy at the end of the row that would be my partner seemed to be the exception to the 'young and reasonably hot' look that the producers had wanted—he was older than the others, had a mane of salt-and pepper curls that went down his back, and the biggest biker beard I'd ever seen. I couldn't read his name because his beard was so long it covered his shirt.

I felt visibly deflated at the sight of him, and my gaze flicked back to Dean, who seemed to be having an equally difficult crisis of decision. He looked at Heidi, then back at me, then back at Heidi again, as if weighing his options.

Oh god. I sure didn't want to be stuck with Dean.

Sure, Old Biker Guy looked like he wouldn't last a week out here, but I'd take him over an arrogant jerk any day. Not that it was my choice to make.

Dean heaved a sigh and put his hands on his oh-so-lean hips, glancing over at Chip the host. I knew he'd made his choice then. His gaze had lingered long and hard on Heidi, and she'd winked at him and given him her best sultry-girl smile. And when he'd looked over at me? I'd glowered at him and crossed my arms over my chest.

"I'll take the pissed off one. Abby." He sounded so thrilled about it too.

I admit, my jaw dropped a little. So did Heidi's.

"Are you sure?" Chip asked, as if he couldn't believe it either.

"Gee, thanks Chip," I called out with an overly sweet voice and stepped off the mat.

"I'm sure," Dean replied, his cocky-guy voice returning, and I gave him my biggest, fakest, most model-ish smile and moved toward him. While Heidi was standing there, I'd do my best to look pleased that I'd been picked. I grabbed my bag and sauntered through the sand—well, with my wet, heavy shoes, it was more like a stumble.

Dean looked chagrined as I wobbled my way over to stand next to him, and Heidi moved to the Old Biker Guy's side, looking equally confused that her hotness had been passed up for the lump of humanity known as myself.

"Welcome to Endurance Island," Chip shouted again, a phrase I was already getting tired of hearing. "Your maps to your camps are tied to your flags. Head there and we'll see you at the next challenge!"

Dean turned and glanced back at me, giving me his lopsided white smile, no doubt carefully calculated to make hearts flutter and panties descend. "Looks like it's just you and me for the next few days."

"Great," I said in a tone of voice that was anything but. "Now do you want to tell me why you picked me instead of Heidi?"

He glanced over at her once, then flicked a dismissive gaze back to me. "She can't swim for shit."

Huh. I have to admit that made me speechless, just a little.

"And besides," he said as he picked up our tribe flag (lucky number eleven). "You're the one with the peanut butter. And now it's *our* peanut butter."

Obviously the peanut butter was a bigger asset camp than I was.

Chapter Three

You know, it's funny. All the other girls on this island look like they'd love to spend a few days alone with me. Abby looks at me as if she'd like to take my axe and gut me like a fish. Weirdest chick I've ever met. Decent swimmer, though. Let's hope she doesn't totally blow it during challenges. —Dean Woodall, Day 2

WE DIDN'T SPEAK AS WE HIKED ALONG THE ISLAND. MYSELF, I couldn't come up with anything civil (and I suspected he had the same problem) so we trekked through the sand and brush in silence. We'd passed by a few other camps—ours was on the far side of the island thanks to our poor number selection. The castaways that had chosen even numbers were hauled off by boat to another nearby island.

Camera-men fluttered in and out of the woods, following us. Since we'd already been instructed to ignore them, I'd done my best to do so. Even now, they were starting to blend in with the scenery, despite the fact that they were constantly jumping a few yards in front of us and filming.

"I see the camp up ahead," Dean said eventually, and I lifted my head to look where he was pointing. Sure enough, a red flag with a bright 11 fluttered near the beach. As we came upon the flag, I frowned. Endurance island was truly going to be an endurance, all right. The flag was planted in the sand in the middle of nowhere, and the only thing that told us that this was our camp was a small cast-iron cook pot and a tiny bag of rice next to it.

Dean paused at the sight of it as well. "Home sweet home, I suppose." He glanced backward at me.

I bit my lip. It was either that, or start screaming.

"I guess the budget must have been cut for this season," I joked. "No four-star resort for us."

"This is about endurance and surviving against the elements," Dean replied in a scathing voice. "What did you expect?"

I glared at the back of his head as he tromped off through the bushes. "Asshole." This was going to be the longest two months of my life, easily.

Despite the jerkoff that was my partner, they couldn't have picked a lovelier location for the filming. Gentle waves lapped against the shore, and the sand that edged the water was smooth and pale and seamless. Palm trees rustled overhead, swishing in the wind coming off of the water, and all around me was the green of vegetation and the blue of the ocean. It was lovely.

Dean was nowhere to be found. Our cameraman had run down the beach to try and find him—it was just me.

Paradise. I smiled and drank in the air.

Of course, the whole 'paradise' realization left me when, after admiring the setting sun for a few minutes, I noticed rain clouds in the distance. And realized that as pretty as our small cove was, there was also zero shelter to be found. My stomach started to growl.

We had no fire. No shelter. My small bag of clothing was soaked, my shoes were squishing on my feet, and I was terribly thirsty. Time to set up camp, I supposed. I picked a somewhat-protected spot with a few over-hanging trees and used a fallen branch to rake the sand, trying to clean out a wide enough spot clear of debris for a fire and a shelter. By the time that was done, I was sweating and dirty and gross, and had managed to clear off a decent-sized spot.

Dean sauntered back at some point, and stood in the distance, watching me. He held a crude bucket in his hands. "I found the water well." He held it out to me. "Brought you a drink."

I eyed him uneasily. That was almost too nice of him to be believed. "Thanks," I said in a cool voice, and took the bucket from him. "Is it safe to drink?"

"I'll find out in about a half hour," he said with a half-grimace.

Fair enough. I took a few cautious sips, then returned it to him. "We should try and boil the rest, just to be on the safe side."

"And what are we going to boil it with?" he asked, taking the bucket back from me. "Our hands? Magic?"

"How about that nasty temper of yours?" I snapped back. "It seems to be boiling over a lot lately."

"Well, can you blame me?" He gave me a disgusted look and gestured at our pathetic camp. "I was gone for over an hour and I come back and you haven't even attempted to start a fire of any kind. What exactly have you been doing?"

"Setting up camp!"

He took an over-exaggerated look around and spread his arms wide. "Wow, it looks amazing. I especially like the lodge you've set up. That's incredible."

"Don't be sarcastic, you ass. I was clearing off the sand so we'd have someplace decent to actually set up. If you want to sleep on a bunch of rocks and branches, you're more than welcome to! I, however, am going to finish making a decent shelter."

"Finish! You haven't even started, sweetheart."

"And I never will if you don't leave me alone!" By this time, I was shouting, gesturing in his face as much as he was gesturing in mine. "Why don't you go do something manly and go kill something for dinner?"

That seemed to surprise him. "Why don't we just eat your peanut butter?"

I shook my head. "Absolutely not. That's mine. You got an axe, I got peanut butter."

His mouth curled into a sneer that still made him sexier than he should have been. "Is that how we're going to do it then? What's yours is yours and what's mine is mine?"

"If that's how you want to be, fine! That is exactly how we can do it," I huffed. Fuck him if he thought I was going to share my peanut butter with him, when all he did was yell in my face. "You keep to your side of the camp and I'll keep to mine, and we'll see who's better off, won't we?"

"Works for me." Dean stomped off to the middle of the small area that I'd cleared and dug his heel down in the center. "We'll build our firepit here. You can stay on that side, and I'll stay on the other."

"That's fine with me," I said in my iciest voice. "And are you going to make a fire?"

"Why, no I'm not," he said with a drawl. "I'm going to go see if I can find myself something to eat."

"Fine then!"

"Fine!"

We glared at each other for a minute longer, and then he stormed off again, tearing through the brushy leaves at the outskirts of camp and spraying sand with each furious step he took. As he left, I caught a glimpse of the cameraman, a delighted look on his face as he filmed me standing in camp.

Hell, he'd just caught everything. How embarrassing. My cheeks flushed with color, I turned away and began to head into the brushy jungle to see what I could find.

Dean had taken the axe with him, so I was forced to do everything by hand. I'd managed to find a few fallen tree branches that would be large enough and straight enough to serve as base-boards for the bed I was going to create. I used some more equally long wood that I placed crosswise, forming a really sorry, hard, and uncomfortable bed two feet off the ground. But at least it was off the sand (which I suspected would be crawling with sand fleas and crabs as soon as the sun went down).

To make up for the discomfort of my bed, I grabbed as much loose greenery and palm fronds as I could, stacking them all into a makeshift bed. When I had several feet of padding on the bed, I climbed onto it and tested it out. Just as I had predicted, the palm fronds flattened within an inch or two, and I was left with a moderately fluffy bed. It'd do for now.

By the time the sun had set entirely, I had gathered enough wood for a fire and dug out the fire pit, but I was too tired to even attempt fire on my own. I lay on my narrow bed (just wide enough to fit my body) and stared up at the intensely beautiful stars overhead, using my bag—hard can of peanut butter and all—as a pillow.

It was unnerving to lay in the darkness, all alone, with things inching and creeping and rustling as things on a deserted island were wont to do. I tried not to think about how I didn't have a roof over my head, or any real protection from anything. I supposed I could drag a palm leaf over my head if it rained, but if anything tried to attack? I was pretty much laid out to snack on, a human pu pu platter.

The underbrush rustled in an alarming way and I glanced up from my bed to see Dean returning to camp, flipping the axe in his hands in an almost-frustrated fashion. I couldn't see his face, but his shoulders seemed tense, and I was a little more gleeful than I should have been. He hadn't found anything to eat either. I patted the jar of peanut butter under my ear. I was hungry right now, but not so hungry that I'd break into my stash. It could wait until tomorrow.

He fumbled around in the darkness. "No fire, I see."

"Nope."

I'm sure he wanted to say more, but he didn't. In the distance I saw the small red dots signifying that our camera-man was still there, filming, and I glanced over at Dean again. He was shaking out something long and thick and it rustled like fabric…a blanket? I sat upright on my hard, rustling bed. "Where did you get that?"

In the thick darkness, I could just about make out that he was laying it on the ground underneath him, and then curled up in it to sleep. "It's my prize. You know, like the peanut butter is yours. And just like that, it's not for sharing."

Bastard. I rubbed my arms, covered in goosebumps. At least he had more than a few pink bikinis to wear, and it was getting chilly. Everything else I had was laying out flat, though, as I tried to dry them off for tomorrow. Shoes, pants, everything still had a damp cast to them. "I don't need your blanket," I retorted. "It's not that cold."

"Not yet," he agreed in a too-amiable voice. "Good night."

Irritated, I flopped back down on my palm leaves and tried to get comfortable.

It was the longest, most miserable night of my life. Dean was right— it did get cold. Extremely cold—to the point that I'd put back on all my damp clothing in the hopes that it would help protect me from the elements—not so much. It got even worse somewhere in the middle of the night when the weather broke and it began to sprinkle. My teeth chattered as I shivered on top of the palm leaves.

At least Dean wasn't much better. All night, I could hear him rustling and itching, and I knew that the sand fleas and the crabs and other creepy-crawly things were driving him insane. I doubted he slept much either. Of course, I wasn't about to invite him up on my bed. Screw him. There wasn't enough room anyhow, and I wasn't about to hug my enemy close all night, even if he did have a lot of body heat.

Morning crawled around an infinite amount of hours later, and with it, a slight warming to the air. Just enough that my teeth stopped chattering, but not enough to revive me. I felt wrung out and exhausted, and dirty. I glanced over at Dean on the far side of our small camp, and his short hair stuck up at weird angles, and he looked equally as wrung out as I was.

Good. At least I wasn't alone in my misery. He nodded over at something in the distance. "What's that?"

I looked behind me to where he was pointing. Sometime in the middle of the night, someone in the production crew had stolen into our camp. A small red box had shown up on a stump at the edge of camp. I wandered over to it, peeling a damp palm leaf off the back of my leg. "Tribal Summons" the lid read. "Challenge today."

I groaned and threw it back down. "Bad news."

Chapter Four

Something's got to give. Either Abby and I need to start working together, or I'm going to have to kill her and eat her.
That's a joke, by the way. —Dean Woodall, Day 2 Interview

A SMALL BOAT CAME BY TO PICK US UP AND TAKE US TO THE Challenge Island. I wore my tankini and my still water-swollen sneakers (thanks to the rain) and kept my bag between my feet, since the message had instructed for us to bring our possessions.

"Elimination Round," Dean had said, and I didn't bother to let him know that I thought he was right.

We arrived just as the other teams did. Twelve tables were set up at the far end of the beach, each one a different color. Each team walked up to their table and planted their flag, then turned to the host, awaiting instructions.

"Hey everyone! Did we all sleep well?" Chip flashed us a cheerful smile. "How was your first night on the beach?"

"It was marvelous," Shanna drawled on the end. "Leon is a great partner."

"Everyone having a good time with their partners, then?" Chip's gaze swung down the line and focused on me.

"Just peachy," I said in a flat voice.

"Partnership," Chip rang out in a condescending voice. "It's so important in a survival situation, and it is what today's challenge is about! Each team is going to paint a series of pictures on a series of flags that you see before you. These pictures will be items that pertain to the history of the Cook Islands and to the native people. You will have five minutes to complete as many flags as possible, as accurately as possible. A judge will then be brought around, and will determine which two groups have the worst flags. Those two groups will go to Judgment tonight, where the other teams will decide which one to vote out. Understood?"

We nodded our understanding, and Chip continued. "Here's how this works. One person on the team will be blindfolded. That person will be the painter. The other will be the caller, who, when I say go, will tear open a sealed packet to uncover the pictures. The caller will then describe each picture to their partner. You must work together," he emphasized, and repeated it again just in case we were dumb. "You *must* work together. Partnership is the key to this challenge. I'll give you all a moment to strategize."

Dean glanced over at me. "You any good with a paintbrush?"

I glared. "Why do I have to be the one to paint? Because I'm the girl?"

He gave me an exasperated look out of his impossibly blue eyes. And he seemed just as tired and cranky as I was. "Look, can you not bite my head off for just one challenge, please? Is that so very hard?"

"Fine," I agreed, feeling just a teensy bit apologetic that I was being difficult to get along with.

"Good," he emphasized.

And just like that, my goodwill vanished. I ground my jaw as he came around behind me to tie my blindfold, and accidentally snared a few strands of my curly brown hair in the knot. It just irritated me even more, especially now that he was acting smug and high-handed as he tied my arm behind my back and treated me like a child while he did so.

I hated him so much in that moment.

"Are the teams ready to go?" I heard Chip call. I lifted my head, bands of sunlight showing under the thick darkness of the blindfold. The day was getting hot and sweat was starting to make the blindfold stick to my face. I could hear the other contestants moving and whispering to each other, preparing for the competition. A strong, warm hand grabbed my free one and shoved a paintbrush in it. "Here," Dean said quickly.

"Ready!" called Chip. "You will have five minutes at the start of the competition....GO!"

At that, I heard the sound of a dozen paper packets tearing open, and I tilted my head, trying to decipher which one was my partner.

"It's a turtle," Dean's voice yelled in my ear, startling me so badly that I jumped and dropped my brush.

"You scared me-"

"Pick up your brush! Pick up your brush!" Dean's voice took on an impatient edge. "I can't pick up your brush for you, Abby. Pick up your brush! It's on the ground!"

Yeah, we were off to a *great* start. With my free hand, I knelt below the table, feeling around. No brush.

"Hurry up, Abby," my partner said helpfully. "You need to draw this goddamn turtle."

"I can't find the brush," I told him, trying to be patient.

"It's on the ground—"

"I'm on the ground, you ass, and I can't find it. Where on the ground? I'm blindfolded, remember?"

He paused for a moment. "Left of your hand," he finally instructed. "Now hurry up and grab it!"

After another infinitely long moment of searching, I felt the smooth length of the brush and wrapped my fingers around it, jumping up...and smacking the back of my head into the table so hard I almost blacked out. Pain shot through my head, and stars lit in front of my eyes. I groaned in pain.

"Get up here! Come *on*!"

I shook it off and made a mental note to kill him. Slowly, I pulled myself back up again and tried to refocus. People were shouting and talking all around me, making it hard to concentrate on Dean's grating voice.

"Turtle," he repeated, his voice urgent. "Draw a turtle."

I slapped the brush down onto the fabric and drew a circle.

"There's no paint on your brush," he barked into my ear. "You need paint for the turtle! Green paint!"

I was starting to see why this was a teamwork challenge and not just for kicks. Irritated, I touched the ends of the brush-bristles. Dry as a bone. "So where is the paint?"

"To your side," he said. "Left, left, left," he chanted as my hand reached for the paint. There was nothing for long, long seconds and then I found a big cup of something wet. I picked up my brush and started to dip it in.

"Wrong color," Dean barked. "That's red!"

"You're supposed to tell me where to go, you idiot," I yelled back at him. "I'm blindfolded—I can't see the colors!"

"You need to ask, then!"

"I'm asking now!"

"And I'm telling you, *not that one*! Move up two pots!"

Oh sure! Easy for him to say. Gritting my teeth, I brushed my knuckles along the edges of the pots until I felt like I'd picked the right one, and moved the brush inside again.

"I said green! That's blue! You're over too far! Two pots, not three."

Argh. Clenching my hand tightly around the brush, I shoved it into the paint. "You're slopping it everywhere," Dean complained in a rather impatient voice. "They're going to count off for that."

"I'm trying," I said, and drew a circle on the fabric. "What is the turtle doing in the picture?"

"It has waves over its head, so you'll need blue paint...no, not yet, you haven't finished the turtle. Draw the legs, and draw the mouth open... open...I said open...Abby, the mouth is open..."

"—I'm drawing it open—"

"No you're not—"

"You have one minute left, teams," Chip broke in, yelling over the constant murmur. "Work fast!"

The fabric ripped out from under my brush. "Move on," Dean said irritably. "Go to the next one."

I felt him lay down a new flag of fabric and patted it flat. "What do I draw for this one?"

"A red fish. Come on Abby, draw fast. A red fish—"

"Where's the red—"

"Abby, hurry up and draw—"

"I can't draw if you don't tell me—"

"ABBY, DRAW," Dean shouted, blasting my ears. "PICK RED AND DRAW. QUIT ASKING SO MANY QUESTIONS AND JUST DRAW."

I threw down my brush, grabbed the closest pot of paint, and lobbed it over the table at my partner. I didn't hear it connect, so I grabbed the next one, and the next one, and heard the satisfying thwacks as they hit Dean (I hoped).

"Time!" Chip shouted.

I ripped off my blindfold and glared at my partner. Mister Perfect Jock was covered in yellow and red paint—quickly dripping to orange. A streak of blue covered half the table and our flag looked as if the paint had thrown up on it. He was glaring at me with utter disgust.

"If you yell at me again," I screamed back, "I'm going to shove that fucking brush down your throat. Understand?"

He glared at me and wiped paint off of his face, saying nothing. A muscle ticked in his jaw but to my relief, he didn't say anything back to me. Instead, he turned and faced Chip, awaiting further instructions.

The others were staring at the two of us in shock, the camera-men buzzing around. They were having a field day—no wonder. Dean and I were a classic example of how not to work together.

"Everyone please sit down with your partners, and we'll have the judges brought in," Chip said in a calm voice. In pairs, the contestants began to move over to the crude wooden benches left nearby, and I followed. Dean stalked behind me, his paint-covered clothing slapping against his body. As we walked over to the designated area, my fury gave way to embarrassment.

We were acting like children.

The embarrassment grew worse when the native judges were brought in, and the flags were held up for each one to see. The other teams hadn't done so badly—one even managed to paint all four designs, though in a very haphazard fashion. When they got to our table, the judges looked over at the two of us sitting on the edge of our bench, turned away from each other, my partner dripping yellow paint, and began to whisper. They held up our first flag—a green circle with a big line slashed through it from where Dean had jerked the fabric out while I was still painting—and shook their heads. The next flag they held up was just a series of red and yellow and blue blotches. Shook their heads again. Snickers arose from the other contestants.

My cheeks flushed with embarrassment again. I glanced over at Dean.

He looked over at me, too, wiped a handful of paint off of his shirt, and then smeared it all over my arm.

Jerk.

"The judges have decided upon the worst teams, and have picked two. Please stand up and move forward with your partner if I call your team's number." Chip turned and looked directly at me. "Team Eleven, you have been nominated for Judgment."

Well, no surprise there. I got to my feet and approached the small area designated as 'Judgment'. I stood in front of a coconut-decorated podium, and Dean did the same.

"Team number Four, you have been nominated for Judgment."

I hadn't even paid attention to the other team's flags. All were equally bad in my opinion, though none to the grand level that ours was. The other team moved forward, looking surprised and a little bit ashamed that their entry was judged almost as bad as ours.

Heck, I would be too.

They moved to the other podiums across from us, and Chip took a seat on the high stool in the middle, as some sort of bizarre island court. The rest of the teams were arranged in a semicircle surrounding us, and a chalkboard and chalk was handed to each team.

"Welcome to our first Judgment Day," Chip announced in a bombastic voice. "Today, we will decide the fate of one of these two teams. We will hear from each team, and then the 'safe' teams that make up our jury will vote for the team they wish to continue. Remember that for now, you are voting to keep a team 'IN'. Later, you will be voting individuals out. Does everyone follow?"

The others nodded enthusiastically.

"Let's start with Team Eleven," Chip said, and swung his gaze over to my podium, and then Dean's. "Do you have any idea of why you two performed so poorly in the challenge?"

"It's his fault—" I began.

"She's impossible—" he started to say at exactly the same moment.

A snicker arose from our audience, and I turned to glare at Dean again. He was giving me the same clenched-jaw look as before. After a moment, I began to speak, still facing him. "We cannot seem to agree on anything, Chip. That's it, pure and simple."

Dean added, "We don't even have camp set up yet."

"Don't tell them that," I snapped. "That's no one's business but ours."

Dean just gave me a quelling look.

Chip seemed surprised. Okay, perhaps a little gleeful that we were self-destructing so abominably. "Did you two manage to get fire yet?"

"Haven't tried," Dean said.

"Food?"

"Nope," I said, and turned to glare at Dean again. If he mentioned my peanut butter in front of the others, I'd kill him. It was my ace in the hole at the moment.

He remained silent.

"Is that why you threw paint on Dean, Abby?" He definitely sounded smug now.

I gave the host a bared-teeth smile. "He was yelling at me and being unhelpful, Chip. So, yes, that's why I threw paint on him."

"She was asking too many questions," Dean butted in. "She wouldn't just shut up and paint—"

"How am I supposed to paint when I am not getting instructions from my partner?"

"What did I tell you, Chip? Impossible." Dean just gave me his winningest smile, as if that would warm me to his argument. "I try my best but she doesn't want to listen."

Chip put his hands in the air. "Okay, okay, thank you, Team Eleven, but I think we've heard enough."

Over in the audience, Shanna was casting meaningful looks at Dean. She wasn't the only one, either. The other girls looked at him as if they wanted to save him from me. No one was giving me the same kind of look, of course. I was just an extra, an obstacle preventing them from having six weeks of unfettered bliss with good ol' Dean. And I had no doubt that they'd take me out as soon as they could.

The host turned to the other team, Vera the gymnast and Sidney that I hadn't had the chance to meet yet. Sidney seemed nice enough, with warm brown hair and a bright smile. Vera too. "So tell me," Chip began, "Is your team having trouble like Team Eleven is?"

"Oh no," Vera said hastily. "We're doing just fine. Sid and I get along great."

As if to prove this point, Sid nodded and put his hand on his partner's shoulder, to show their solidarity.

I made a face at that, and Dean snorted behind me.

"So why is it that you're here for this round of eliminations?" Chip asked, trying to make his question as serious as possible. He even put his hand under his chin, as if considering a matter of grave importance.

Sid shrugged his shoulders and glanced down at Vera. "I think we just got unlucky. That's all."

"And how is life back at camp?"

"We're doing good," Sid continued, and his smile widened. "We have fire, and Vera was able to find us some coconuts last night. We're doing all right."

I rolled my eyes. Impossible to believe that everyone was getting along well except for myself and Dean. We were put into these kinds of situations deliberately to self-destruct, I imagined. No one was going to get along as blissfully as Vera and Sid were playing up.

Chip chatted with them for a moment more, then turned to the teams in the audience. "It's now decision time. We're going to have each team move to the voting booth and cast their ballot for the team that they wish to vote off Endurance Island." He gestured at the far end of the row. "Team Number One, you're up first."

Shanna and Leon hopped to their feet, slate in hand, and disappeared into a small curtained off booth in the background. I squinted at the sun, high overhead, and wondered how much longer this would take.

I mean, it was obvious that they'd be writing our number down. We were a complete and total train-wreck of a team. There was no way Dean and I would get anywhere if we didn't learn to get along, and so far, we *weren't* learning.

A pair at a time, the others went up to vote until no one was left. Chip disappeared off to the side and returned with a box decorated to look as if it were a missing crate of supplies to go with the shipwreck theme. Very clever. He scanned us again—participants and people on the hot seat—and then pulled the lid off.

"First vote…"

I closed my eyes. My book deal, my job, everything. I could smell it going down the drain.

"Team Four."

I clenched my gut, and then took a breath in surprise. Wait, that was the other team. Why was someone voting for them? We were terrible.

Chip pulled out the next slate, then turned it around so we could all see it. "Team Four."

It didn't make sense…did it? I watched Shanna's impassive face, Ginger's, Jody's…and they all wore the same inexpressive look.

"Team Four."

Someone's mouth curled up slightly, and it struck me. Of course. It was blindingly obvious now. They wanted to keep us here because we sucked.

We couldn't work together—which made us no threat. And Team Four, because they were marginally more competent than us, would go home.

"Team Four," Chip continued, flipping over another slate, and then another. "Team Four. Team Four. Five out of nine votes…that's enough." He nodded at Team Four's shocked faces and banged a gavel against a coconut. "Endurance Island has passed Judgment. Your time here is over." He turned and glanced over at myself and Dean. "You are safe for one more round. Head back to camp."

Stunned, I glanced over at Dean to see his expression. He seemed just as shocked as I was.

And here I'd thought we'd get voted out first because we were the worst team out there. The worst team possible. Just the opposite was true—we were going to be kept around as dead weight, as a safe bet.

Even though I wasn't supposed to, I smiled a little. I'm pretty sure Dean did too.

Chapter Five

You know, if I didn't want to wring her neck on a constant basis, I'd say Abby is a really cute girl. More of a Mary Ann than a Ginger, but I've always had a thing for Mary Ann.
—Dean Woodall, Day 3

As soon as we got back to camp, Dean tossed his bag onto the sand. "I'm going to take a walk," he said, and turned away before I had a chance to answer.

I sat down my bag and relaxed in the warm sand for a few minutes, wiggling my toes in the grains. I glanced backward at our small camp, and my spirits deflated. We had a fire pit, but no fire. I had a makeshift platform for a bed, but no cover. We didn't have anything to eat, or drink.

Some paradise.

I found a couple of coconuts by trekking through the woods, but discovered that Dean had taken the axe with him. Stomach grumbling, throat dry, I realized I didn't even know where the well was. With no way to eat the meager food, and not quite ready to delve into my peanut butter stash yet, I decided to work on my shelter.

All I really needed to make my small shelter complete was some sort of cover to protect from the wind (and rain, if I should be so unlucky). I decided on a small A-frame, since that seemed the easiest to make, and set about to creating it. The wood was easy enough to find, though I didn't have anything to lash it together with…I ended up using my pink string bikini to hold the frame together. Like I was going to wear that. Shelter was far more important. I dove into my task with single-minded determination.

By the time I glanced up, the sun was going down, I was covered in sweat and bug bites, and I hadn't given a single thought to making fire. But my small shelter was done! I felt a sense of pride as I looked at the small thing, and glanced over at the blanket that stuck out of Dean's pack with a smug sense of pride. One of us would be sleeping well tonight, and even though he had a blanket, I had a shelter.

I gathered some wood and tinder to make a fire, but the sun was too low into the sky and I couldn't see what I was doing—I was mostly guessing at this point anyhow. Dean was still nowhere to be seen, and I stared longingly at my coconuts, still covered in the tough green casing. I could try and split one against a fallen tree, but if I busted it, I'd lose all the good milk inside it. Even though I was trembling with hunger, I forced myself to wait, cradling it in my arms and sliding into my shelter with my backpack to wait for Dean's return.

I must have fallen asleep at some point—I started awake when I felt something warm and heavy touch my feet. "What—"

"Take my blanket," Dean said in a gruff voice, shoving it onto my legs. "Your teeth are chattering so hard I can't sleep."

I hadn't realized how cold I was until he'd tossed the blanket over me, and I snuggled under it gratefully. "What about you?" I asked sleepily. "My shelter isn't big enough for both of us."

"Don't worry about me. I can't sleep anyhow," Dean said, and I heard him walking away.

Morning came when I could no longer deny the gnawing hollow of my stomach with sleep. I crawled out of my shelter, coconut in hand, staring blearily up at the sky. Still morning, but not early. The sun was high.

Dean sat a distance away on the sand, his shoulders rolled slightly as he hunched over something. He looked…tired. Even from this angle. It gave me a twinge of guilt to see that, and I approached slowly with my coconut in hand. Part of me wanted to hide it, but he'd been generous enough to share his blanket with me—the least I could do is offer to share my food.

If I had to.

He didn't glance over at me as I approached, fixated on his task, and I peered over his shoulder. He had sticks in hand, his shoelaces tied to a bowed stick and was trying to rub them together to make fire. He was doing it completely wrong. Judging from the sweat on his forehead, he'd also been at it for a while.

My stomach growled and I decided to skip pointing out the obvious, moving around him and looking for the axe. It sat on the far side of his left leg, half covered in sand a few feet away, and I moved to pick it up. "Morning."

He grunted something that might have been a hello, not looking up from his task. With the bow and string, he sawed back and forth on another stick of wood, obviously trying to make fire. Doing a damned pitiful job of it too.

I hefted the axe and examined my coconut, trying to determine the best way to open it. I had no friggin clue. After a moment, my hunger won out and I simply dropped it on the ground a fair distance away and lifted the axe.

"You're going to hurt yourself," Dean said behind me. "Especially if you hold the axe like that."

I bristled at that and turned to glare at him. "I'm starving and this coconut is going into my stomach in the next five minutes, or I am going to have to go after small woodland creatures with this axe. Got it?"

I could have sworn that his mouth twitched at that. "I saw the other coconut you left out for me last night—thanks." He stood up and brushed the sand off of his swim trunks and moved over to stand beside me, his hand out for the axe. "Let me do it."

A scowl touched my face, and I glared at him even harder, hugging the axe to me. "Is this some sort of macho bullshit?"

"No, this is a I-really-don't-want-to-have-to-bandage-you-up sort of bullshit. It took me forever to figure out how to crack mine open, and your hands are shaking. Now give it to me or you're going to hurt yourself."

Reluctantly, I handed over the axe. He had a point, and my hands were indeed shaking like leaves. I moved back a couple of feet so he could split open my coconut for me, but still hovered nearby, watching closely. I didn't want to take my eyes from it, for fear that this was a trick and he'd run off and eat my food.

But it seemed that I was more suspicious than he was. With easy, sure movements, he peeled the green husk from the coconut and used one tip of the axe to chop a hole at the top of the coconut, and then held it out to me. "Drink that. When you're done drinking it, I'll crack it open for you."

With overjoyed fingers, I snatched the nut from his hands and raised it to my mouth. The first sweet mouthful touched my lips and I wanted to pass out at the sheer heaven of it. Wet and sugary, it was the best thing I'd ever tasted. I took another thirsty gulp and then glanced over guiltily at Dean. It took everything I had to hold out the coconut and offer him a drink. "Did you want some?"

He waved me off. "Nah. I had three of them this morning."

"Three?" I sputtered, anger surging past my guilt. "Where did you get three?"

Dean gave me an odd look, the I'm-stuck-here-with-the-crazy-girl glance I'd come to recognize so well in the past two days. "We're on a tropical island. They're everywhere. You can have three for breakfast if you want, too."

Right. I hadn't realized. Hunger was making me faint—and stupid. Of course there were coconuts on the island. I didn't know why it hadn't occurred to me to look for more. Exhaustion, I supposed. We had rice, too—once we figured out how to boil it.

I tipped my head back and finished draining the coconut, disappointed when it was empty and I had to hand it back. A moment later, Dean split it with an easy crack of the axe, and handed the two halves back to me. I crammed the thick white meat into my mouth as fast as I could. Oh god, it was so good and my stomach was so empty.

Dean moved back to his fire building supplies and took up the bow again, his shoulders setting in the same resigned stance that I'd seen before. I said nothing as I scooped and ate, scooped and ate. He picked up the bow and begin to saw at the wood again, the sticks twisting back and forth with great speed…and little results.

When I'd pried the last ounce of coconut from the empty husk and licked my fingers clean—gritty sand and all—I watched Dean for a moment more. His face was dripping with sweat, his movements exhausted but steady.

"You're doing it wrong," I decided to blurt out despite my better judgment.

He lifted his head, squinted at me and swiped at his forehead with one hand. His mouth set in a hard line. "What do you mean, I'm doing it wrong?"

I crawled over in the sand, moving to the other side, and pushed his hands away from the fire-making implements so I could study them easier. It was obvious to me where he'd gone wrong. "Here," I said, and pointed at his bottom stick, where he'd carved a small hole to catch the spark. "You need some tinder and then cut a notch here for the ember."

Dean tried to take it back from me. "Listen, I have—"

I held it away from him. "Can you just trust me and do it, already?"

We glared at each other for a few moments, and then he got up and headed down the beach to get a palm leaf. By the time he returned, I had a notch cut into the wood and began to set everything back up again—wood, coconut fluff for tinder, and the leaf itself. I set everything in place and then handed him the bow again. "You want to do it, or do you want me to?"

"By all means," he said with a gesture. "Go ahead."

Clearly he expected me to fail. I snorted at that and positioned the bow, then set to work.

If you've ever made a fire out of sticks, well, you know it's not an easy task. You have to get the friction going really well, and that means sawing very hard, which also means sawing very fast. My arm was screaming after about thirty seconds, but I wasn't about to give up. Instead, I ignored the sweat beading on my brow, bit my lip, and continued to continually move the bow back and forth, trying to coax a spark from the implements.

And after what seemed like eternity, a small plume of smoke rose. "You got it!" Dean yelled in my ear, and leaned in to blow on the small kernel of fire. It flared and we hastily shoved the fire-making sticks aside, adding more bits of dried coconut husks to try and keep it going. And when it was a real flame, Dean wrapped the entire thing in the palm leaf and carried it back to our fire pit, placing the smoking bit at the bottom of the wood pile with delicate hands. I followed behind him, wiping my brow.

"How did you know?" He glanced over at me, then turned back to blow on the flame some more.

"Know what?" I said. "How to build the fire?"

He shook his head, not taking his eyes off the firepit as he fed the flickering flame more and more tinder, and small sticks of wood. "I've been trying since last night. I rubbed those sticks for so long and so hard I thought my arms would fall off, and you managed to do it in twenty minutes."

I moved closer to the building fire, pleased that he'd been so struck by my efforts. "I reviewed a book for a celebrity survivalist once. Very big deal for the publisher, and the guy was a total asshole. He wrote it himself instead of having his ghostwriter do it, or so he told me. Anyhow, he was a real jerk, so I hired a wilderness survival guide and we went through each 'survival' tip in the guide. And I gave him an "F"." I nodded at the fire, my mouth curving into a smile in remembrance. "He got the whole fire-making thing wrong too. Same reason—that stupid notch at the bottom."

Dean shook his head at me, his mouth not quite curving into a smile. "You just love proving people wrong, don't you Abby?"

I didn't respond, but I didn't need to. The smile on my face was enough. It felt good to smile after three days of complete and utter misery, and I got a funny, warm feeling in my stomach when Dean smiled back, his own mouth moving into a slow and devastating curve.

God, why did I have to get stuck with such a beautiful—and arrogant—man?

To distract him from the look he was casting in my direction, I nodded at the fire. "I can take care of it."

Dean glanced over at the stump with our Tribal Summons. "We have mail, you know."

I groaned at that. "Again today?"

He nodded. "Probably some sort of reward challenge. The boat should be here soon." He glanced over at me, blue eyes focused on my face, so vivid against his dark tan. "I think we need to have a serious talk before we go, however."

I wanted to groan at that. We were being civil adults for the moment, and it was a nice change. I didn't want to go back to hating him just yet. It was far too exhausting. "Do we have to?"

"Look. We're both here because we want to win. I think we need to reconsider our...tactics."

I had to smile reluctantly at that. "What, you mean screaming at each other is not exactly going to get us to the end?"

A hint of a smile tugged at his mouth as well. "Something like that. We need to work together if we're going to make it to the very end. If we keep ending up at the bottom of the heap, we're going to get knocked off, no matter how much of a train wreck we seem to be."

I nodded at that. He had a very good point.

"I hate losing, and I think that we'd be a good team if we could just get it through our hard heads that we need to work together—"

I began to roll my eyes at him. "You don't need to butter me up—"

"I'm serious," he interrupted me again, and gestured at the fire he was slowly feeding. "Look what we've accomplished in a short hour. We've eaten, we've got fire, and we can boil our water. You have a shelter, but you're still freezing at night. I have a blanket but no shelter, so I'm warm and covered in bug bites from sand fleas." He paused to scratch his arm, as if emphasizing his point. "The point is, neither one of us is sleeping."

I remained silent at that, thinking about how well I'd slept last night with his borrowed blanket. The blanket that he'd given to me. He'd gone and walked the beach the entire night, probably trying to keep warm, and spent the morning trying (unsuccessfully) to build a fire. Yeah, we weren't exactly rocking Endurance Island with our skills.

At my silence, he sighed. "Look, Abby, I realize you've gotten into your head that you don't like me because I'm a handsome, athletic guy—"

I sputtered at that, my goodwill towards him teetering dangerously towards zero.

"—But you can hate me after the game, when one of us has won two million dollars."

"I don't hate you," I protested. "But you didn't exactly endear yourself to me when you stepped on me to swim your way to shore and win, you know."

"Was that you?" He grinned widely. "Oops."

I clenched my jaw. Half of me wanted to sock him in the face—old, cocky Dean—but the other part of me wanted to laugh at the boyish smile he wore as he glanced up at me over the fire. To me, that seemed to be new Dean. The Dean I was going to be living and sleeping with for the next six weeks.

Sad to say, but in the past hour, I had really warmed up to new Dean. I scratched at my bug bites and gave him a small, reluctant shrug. "All right. We can work together."

He nodded. "What's mine is yours and what's yours is mine. I'll stop hiding the axe and the map to the water well."

My jaw dropped. "You were hiding stuff?"

Dean grinned and gave me an innocent look. "You're hiding your peanut butter, aren't you?"

I bristled at that. "The peanut butter is pure protein and sugar. I'm saving it," I began, and then choked on the words when his expression changed. Sigh. "We need to save it," I corrected myself. "For when we're tired and exhausted and a challenge is coming up."

"You mean like today?" He said and squinted at the shore. In the distance, a small red boat was pulling up, and I knew we were going to rush off to the challenge soon.

He did have a point, though. Even after a belly-full of coconut, I was still weak and shaky and he looked exhausted too. We could use a little energy before the challenge, and to cement our deal together. So I got up, brushing the sand off my bottom and glanced over at the boat.

Dean cursed under his breath. "Man, they have shit timing, don't they? Just when we got our fire started."

I moved toward the shelter, gesturing at a massive log I'd dragged over the other day. "Put that big hunk of wood over the fire. It'll smolder and keep it burning."

"More tips from that book?"

I smiled as I ducked into my makeshift shelter, digging for my bag. "Never piss me off."

"Boy, no kidding." But his laugh was admiring. "What are you doing?"

I pulled the peanut butter jar out of my bag and brandished it. "Cementing our alliance of two with a goodwill gesture," I said, and when he reached for the jar, I pulled it out of his reach again. "Not so fast there, buddy. We need to parcel this out and make it last if we're going to be taking hits before every challenge."

I expected him to bitch about it, or get ugly with me, but his mouth only curled into that amused smile that made the corners of his eyes crinkle. Damn, his eyes were really blue, especially under the bright sunlight. "You're the boss," was all he said.

With deliberate, almost shaking fingers, I screwed off the cap of the peanut butter jar and removed the protective seal. A thin layer of peanut oil covered the top. The scent wafting up from the jar—roasted peanuts and oil—made my stomach growl, and Dean gave a small, deep moan. "Damn, that smells good," he said.

I nodded and glanced around—the only sticks we could use for scooping out the peanut butter were covered in sand and camp filth, so I decided to use the next best thing. I stuck my dirty finger in my mouth and sucked all of the grit off of it, and then carefully dug into the jar with my somewhat-clean finger. After all, my mouth was probably the cleanest thing on this island at the moment. With careful precision, I scooped a glop of the chunky peanut butter onto my finger, the mound glistening, and held it out to Dean. Just a small amount, a tablespoon at the most. Just enough to stave off hunger pains and give us a burst of energy.

My thought was to hold out the peanut butter so he could transfer it to his own finger. Perhaps the sight of me sucking on my finger before had distracted him, because he leaned in and took my finger in his mouth, rasping his tongue against it.

And just like that, the world flipped.

Heat rushed through me at the feel of his tongue against my finger, his hot mouth sucking on my skin. I forgot about the peanut butter that was his original goal and my body flushed, my mind skidding to a halt at the sight of his beautiful mouth over my skin, the feel of his tongue against my flesh. I must have shivered or tried to pull away, because his hand grasped my own and held me there as he lapped and rasped against my finger, cleaning my skin.

Searing me to my core.

A wave of heat pulsed through my body and I inhaled sharply. Dean's gaze moved to my face, and I knew that he was realizing the same thing I was. His tongue moved slowly against my skin, sensually. His eyes were locked on my own, and his tongue gave my finger one last flick that I felt all the way down to my sex. Then he released my hand. "Sorry."

"It's okay," I said in a daze, my gaze still locked on his mouth.

He nodded at the shore and stepped past me, clearing his throat. "Boat's here."

In a daze, I stared down at my finger and wondered if I could put it in my own mouth after that...or would it be dangerously close to kissing him?

Our team dynamic had changed again. I touched my finger to my lips and stared after Dean thoughtfully.

Chapter Six

*I have no idea why I licked the peanut butter off of her finger.
One moment she's just standing there, taunting me, and the next,
I've got her finger in my mouth and I'm licking her with my tongue
and I'm getting turned on. And now I can't stop looking
at the way her butt looks in those bikinis.*
—Dean Woodall, Day 4

"WELCOME TO TODAY'S CHALLENGE," SAID CHIP AS THE TEAMS FILED in and moved to stand on our numbered mats. When we were in place, he continued. "Today's challenge is going to be a Luxury Challenge. Teams will compete in the race today, and instead of the bottom two being marked for Judgment, the rules are a little different. This time, the bottom five teams will not be eligible to win a reward. The teams that place in the top six of the event will be. Understand?"

We nodded our agreement, and my eyes kept straying out to the course. I could see a table from where I stood behind Dean. The tables were set up on the edge of the lagoon, and in the water I could see colorful, numbered floats bobbing out in the distance. It sure looked like a lot of swimming. My stomach clenched a little at the thought. Dean was great at swimming. I was not. And if I lost this for us, would our tenuous agreement to not kill each other end?

I liked being on Dean's side, oddly enough.

For some reason, I kept picturing his mouth on my hand, and the feel of his tongue against my skin. I blushed at the memory and forced myself to concentrate on what Chip was saying.

Chip pointed out at the water. "Each colored buoys has a bag of puzzle pieces underneath. One partner will swim out to grab the bag. Once you have a bag, swim to shore and turn it over to your partner. You need five bags total. The other partner will use the puzzle pieces to solve their board and raise their team's flag. The first six teams to raise their flags win a prize. Want to see what you're playing for?"

I nodded and clapped my hands as eagerly as the others. After a few nights of being stuck on a barren beach, we were all excited at the prospect of luxury items.

Chip slowly pulled a decorative box off of the first plate. "Matches," he called out, and held it aloft.

We clapped—who wouldn't want matches when you had to build your fire by hand?

The next two items were shown—food. One plate had sandwiches, and the next had cookies. I heard a collective groan from the girls at the sight of the cookies. I had to admit that chocolate sounded pretty good right now.

The next few items were equally good—a blanket and a set of pillows. The last item to be revealed was the one that truly caught my attention. Chip lifted the final box and displayed a large dark-green bottle. "Something for the skin," he announced. "A native bug repellent made from eucalyptus oil."

Just hearing that made me scratch, and I glanced up at Dean, who was having the same reaction I was. Bug repellent would be very nice.

"Line up, teams, and let's get ready!" Chip lifted his arm in the air, and we sprung into action.

It didn't take much convincing for me to agree that Dean would be our swimmer. He nodded at me and moved out to the edge of the beach with the other men, and I stood behind our table, sizing up who else was working the puzzles. All the female partners had been left to do the puzzles except for ex-military Ginger, who was moving down to swim with the guys. If anyone could do it, it was her, I acknowledged with a wry smile.

I glanced down at my puzzle-board, noting the edges. The colors were striated in a zebra pattern that consisted of several different colors. It was supposed to be confusing, but that would actually make matching up the pieces easier. The best thing to do would be to create the edges and build in from the middle. Confident, I glanced down the line at the others designated with the puzzles. They weren't even looking at their boards, but staring at the male partners. The men were stripping down to their swim trunks, and it was an impressive display of bronzed male flesh. Several eyes, I noted, seemed to be focused on my partner in particular and his rock hard body with the abs that you could bounce a quarter off of.

Not that I had noticed, of course.

"Contestants ready?" Chip raised his arm in the air, raising up a flag with the green Endurance Island logo on it. "Set...Go!"

Dean was the first one in the water, his muscular legs pumping as he splashed into the water until it was waist high, and then doing a half-dive into the water. Those of us waiting on the beach cheered our partners on—well, except for me. I didn't want to cheer for Dean in front of the others. They were still giving us smirking looks, clearly expecting the two of us to self-destruct again. For some reason, that made me feel safe. They didn't know of our little deal to try and get along, and they clearly didn't see us as a threat. So I didn't cheer him, just stood at my table with my fists clenched, my body a nervous pillar of tension.

The swimmers began to immediately tackle their first buoys, but Dean swam further out, to the far end of the lagoon, heading towards the furthest piece. I bit my lip at the sight, but realized that he was making a very smart move—when he was tired and the race was down to the wire, he wouldn't have as far to swim.

Others began to notice too, and as the first puzzle pieces were handed off, I could hear scolding from the other partners. "Get the ones out farthest first! Go! Hurry!"

But they had their puzzle pieces in hand and I did not, so I was forced to stand on our mat and wring my hands, waiting for Dean to arrive again. We were far behind the others at this point, but I saw a couple adjusting their strategy and knew it would all make up in the end—I hoped. Some of the others were already tackling their puzzles, and all I could do was stare at Dean as he emerged from the water.

And oh my, was he gorgeous when he did. The water glistened off of his rock-hard abdomen and sluiced down his chest, and my mouth went dry when his loose shorts dipped low on his hips. Water dripped from his skin as he raced up to me, and I held out my hands like a marionette. He shoved the bag into my arms and turned around before I could talk to him, running back for the water again, his feet spraying sand in my face.

The moment was over.

I grabbed the puzzle pieces and ripped the bag open, throwing the puzzle pieces down on my board. There were ten pieces in my bag, so fifty altogether. I immediately flipped them and began to separate them by color and edge. Before I could start with the edges, Dean was back and threw another wet bag onto my table, then darted off again, and I started the whole process once more. All around me, people were screaming and running and spraying sand, and it was difficult to concentrate. I bent my head low and continued to sort my puzzle pieces, trying to tune out the others.

Three more times, Dean came and dropped a bag of puzzle pieces on my table, and the third time, he sat down on the mat, breathing hard. Good! Done! We had all of our pieces! I immediately finished sorting them by color and began to grab the ones I'd designated as edges, shoving them into place on the board. I'd been a whiz at puzzles when I was a kid, and a Tetris nerd as a teenager, and this was the same thing, I told myself. I worked rapidly, shoving pieces back and forth, filling in my puzzle by completing each color and working from right to left.

"How did they get all their pieces so fast?" Someone grumbled to the side of me, and I heard low whispering. I didn't dare look up from my puzzle, but the tone of that voice had given me a cold shiver. If we weren't perceived as useless and weak…we wouldn't last long if we got in the bottom again. Not with Dean's impressive athleticism.

I slowed down, shoving a yellow piece in the midst of several pink ones, and began to pretend to think hard, even though my mind was mentally fitting the pieces with ease and I was almost done with the puzzle. I didn't want to be first. It'd be a death-knell for us if we were first.

Water dripped on the edges of my board. "What are you doing?" Dean hissed at me. "Why are you slowing down?" He pointed at one piece, my yellow one. "That doesn't go there."

I looked up and glared at him. "Back off," I demanded in a loud voice, clearly startling my partner. "I know what I'm doing! Leave me alone!" I winked, but I doubted he could see it.

Dean gave me a shocked look, raising his hands in the air. He scowled in my direction, and I quickly shuffled pieces, moving the yellow one back to the proper spot, and glancing down the line. The others were still working hard. Dumb Heidi on the right of me hadn't even gotten the edges of her puzzle built. She wasn't a threat. Damn. I was still too far ahead.

What would be a good place? Fourth? Fifth? I desperately wanted a prize, but I also didn't want to win.

Dean leaned in again. "Abby, what the hell are you doing?"

"Argue with me," I murmured under my breath, sliding another piece in. I had two left in my hand, and I pretended to check the other pieces, as if I wasn't sure that they fit together, glancing down the line. "Just argue with me. Loud," I whispered.

He paused for a moment and it got quiet, and I wondered if he was going to catch on to my request. Then, loudly, "Are you a moron?"

"Go away," I snarled at him, testing another piece and glancing down the line. "You're making me nervous!" Lord, I hoped my acting was convincing.

"I'm trying to win this thing for us and you're slowing me down," Dean shouted, and I winced. "Did you not see that I was ahead? I was winning this thing!"

"Puzzles are hard," I replied in a whiny voice.

"Done!" Someone shouted down the line, and a flag went up. Team Three.

I sucked in a breath, waiting, and slowly pressed in another piece.

"Done," called someone else a moment later. Then another, "Done!" Two more flags rose.

"Abby," Dean said in a warning voice, urgency putting an edge into his tone.

"We're done!" A team close to me shouted, and Team Nine raised their flag.

I slammed the last piece in and flipped the lever on my flag, letting it soar. Screw waiting—I couldn't stand it any longer. Fifth would do. "Done," Dean shouted, a mere moment before one team called out, and then another. We were close, lucky. So lucky.

My heart hammered in my chest at the look Dean gave me.

"Teams Three, Seven, Eight, Nine, Eleven and Two are our lucky winners!" Chip waved the flag.

I heard Heidi snort to my right hand side, and a few people glanced back at us in surprise. Dean looked over at me and his mouth began to cock up in a smile.

I immediately threw one of the wet puzzle bags in his face, mentally wincing at the loud slap the wet fabric made. "Next time, don't yell at me when I'm trying to work," I yelled at the top of my lungs. "Jerkface!"

The teams nearby snickered, and the camera-men immediately moved in like vultures as I stomped my feet and shoved past Dean towards the winner's circle where the other teams were gathering. They were lining up in order, teams hugging and leaning on each other in delight.

Dean moved to my side and I gave him a bit of a shove.

In the order that we finished, the teams got to pick their prizes. No surprise, the matches were the first thing to go. Not that I could blame them—if it would have been my choice, I would have been hard pressed to pass up easy fire. I had my eyes on the bug repellent, though. Already I could feel my skin itching.

The next team picked the cookies, and a collective sigh was heard around the challenge area as they took blissful bites out of them. Then, the sandwiches, followed by the collective sighs. My fingers were crossed tightly as the next team seemed to discuss for a moment. "Blanket," they said, and I exhaled sharply, looking over at Dean.

He didn't even pause. "Bug repellent," he said, and scratched a bug bite on his arm.

Chip nodded and came and awarded the bottle to us. Dean took it from him and tucked it under his arm, deliberately not letting me get close to it, and I had to admit that it hurt my feelings. I glared at his back as the last team was handed their pillows and the small boats began to line up again to take us back to our camp sites.

We didn't speak on the way back to camp—one of the rules of Endurance Island - and it bothered me that Dean wouldn't even look in my direction. Hadn't he understood what I was trying to do? I wanted to ask him, but I waited. And when they had dropped us off at our beach and it was no one but myself and Dean and the cameraman standing on the beach under the midday sun, Dean glanced down at the bottle, then turned and looked at me.

"That was a huge risk, you know."

"I know," I admitted.

He shook his head, a grin slowly sliding across his face. "I don't know whether to scream at you or to kiss you."

For some reason, that admission made me shy, and my mind immediately went back to the peanut butter. I felt my face grow hot—damn—and I gave him a goofy smile. "I was hoping you'd catch on to what I was doing. If the others think we can't work together, we're safe if we happen to come into the final two again. Think about it—they're going to keep us around because we're a liability. We'd be fools not to play that up."

He moved closer and grabbed the back of my head, twisting his hand into my thick, curly hair. For a moment there, I thought he was going to lean in and kiss me, but he only grinned and looked directly into my face, inches away. "You are a genius, you know that?"

This was getting dangerously close to flirting. I shoved at his chest, albeit in a more playful fashion. "I'm just tired of getting eaten by bugs."

"Me too," he agreed, pulling the cork out of the bottle. "But I wouldn't have minded a sandwich. Dean held out the bottle, sniffed it, and then made a face. "Smells strong."

I scratched at the welts on my arms. "Probably to keep the bugs away."

"Waterproof, too, according to the label. That's nice of them, considering they've parked us on a beach." Dean grinned. He tilted the bottle in my direction, offering it to me. "Ladies' first?"

I took the bottle from him and gave it a small sniff, then winced. He was right, it did smell really strong. I poured a small bit onto my hand and felt the texture—thick like lotion. The sand was going to stick to us like mad, but I didn't care. I'd take gritty sand all over me and no bugs. With quick, enthusiastic motions, I began to rub it onto my bare, exposed arms.

Seeing my enthusiasm, Dean poured a small bit into his hand as well and began to cover his body as well. We stood there in the blistering sunlight, rubbing bug repellent lotion on our bodies, giddy with delight. After all, in swimwear there was so much skin uncovered, I suspected we'd end up using the entire bottle up long before the game was over. I didn't care—I wanted relief from bugs now.

I saw Dean's hand slide over his lower back, and noticed a big bare patch where he couldn't quite reach his skin, and imagined the bugs landing there. With my grease-slicked hands, I immediately began to rub the lotion across the span of his back, hitting between his shoulder-blades and down his spine to cover his body in its entirety. Dean grunted at that, and I guessed he was pleased. "Thanks," he said, as I slicked my hands over the rock-hard muscles one last time. "Here," he said, pulling away. "Let me do you."

I turned and presented my back to him, rubbing my hands on my bare stomach and thinking how different my body felt from his. His entire build was one of lean muscle and corded sinew—I was all softness and curves. Embarrassed, I almost stepped away again until I felt his hands slide over my shoulders, slick with lotion. And then I gave a sigh of pure pleasure. Not only would it keep the bugs away, but it was cool and refreshing against my hot, sun-dry skin. I arched and flexed a little under his skimming hands. Nothing should feel quite that heavenly.

After a moment or two, it became clear to me that the lotion-rubbing had proceeded past the 'perfunctory' stage. His hands still slid across my slick back, but the feel had taken on a more exploratory sensation, and I felt his fingertips trail across the dip in the small of my back, sending shivers through my skin. His hands flattened against my lower back, as if spanning my waist, and I sucked in a breath at the sensations that shot through me. They definitely had nothing to do with the game, and everything to do with Dean's nearness. His fingertips moved along my sides, gently skimming in an almost ticklish fashion, trailing upward until I felt them touch against the straps of my bikini top. I felt him move forward a step, his shadow falling over me, and my entire body felt soft and languid, heat coursing through me.

"Abby," Dean began in a low, husky voice, and I turned, gazing over my shoulder at him with heavy-lidded eyes. The look on his face was heated, sexual.

Something crashed in the underbrush nearby. Startled, I pulled away from Dean and averted my face, trying to hide the flush creeping over my face. He cleared his throat, and whatever moment we were having—or about to have—vanished.

Two figures emerged out of the palm trees on the far side of camp and waved at us. I squinted in the bright sunlight, trying to make out their names. "Lana and…Will." Both were dressed in vivid yellow that played well against their dark skin.

"Are they supposed to be here?" I glanced over at my partner.

Dean shrugged, his muscles still gleaming from the lotion. "I guess the camera-man will tell us if not, right?"

The camera-man usually assigned to our beach hovered not too far away—I barely noticed him anymore—and he didn't seem to be having any sort of show-produced anxiety attack, or calling his boss on his satellite phone, so I guessed that the occasional camp visits were allowed.

After a moment's hesitation, I moved forward, following Dean.

Lana was waving cheerfully, a sly smile on her face as we approached, and I guessed that she'd seen Dean and I doing the mutual-lotion-rub-down. Her partner was juggling two coconuts in his arms and held them out as we approached. "Housewarming gift," he declared in an equally cheerful voice.

The two of them were far too happy to see us. It made me uneasy, considering we were playing a competitive game in which one team could easily eliminate the other. Still, as Dean strode forward with an easy grin, his hand out to shake hands with them, I tagged behind, feeling like the reluctant asshole that I'd been cast as.

Lana hugged Dean and pulled away, wrinkling her nose. "What is that you've got all over you?"

Dean grinned and put a hand back down to his greasy chest as I pulled up alongside him, trying to contain my frown. "Sorry, we were trying out our bug repellent."

As I watched, Lana's brown eyes lit up and she reached for Dean again. "In that case, I should rub up against you some more."

My partner side-stepped with a small laugh, and Will grinned, but I couldn't muster the same. I settled for a tight smile that didn't feel as if it belonged on my face.

Another awkward moment passed, and then Lana waved her hands, as if trying to chase away the awkwardness. "We wanted to see if you guys had fire and we could borrow some, since we're practically neighbors."

"We have food," Will added, holding up the coconuts. "And two bananas." He pulled them out from his shirt.

I have to admit, I gasped in delight at that. "There are bananas on this island?"

"And mango, if you know where to look," Lana said, smiling. "We can show you if you promise not to show anyone else. In exchange for fire, of course."

I glanced over at Dean, and he looked at me. "Can you give us a second?" I asked, and before anyone could answer, grabbed my partner by the elbow and dragged him away.

"What do you think?" Dean whispered low in my ear. The feel of his breath against my neck made my entire body shiver with want.

"I'm not sure," I admitted, still a little irritated at the sight of beautiful

Lana rubbing her hands over Dean's chest. Why that bothered me, I couldn't quite say. I mean, Will was good-looking too, but I wasn't getting hot and bothered by the thought of Lana putting her hands on him.

"If they can show us where the rest of the fruit is—"

"I know, but fire?" I shrugged my shoulders, then crossed my arms over my chest. "What if we're the only ones that have fire? How much of an advantage are we giving away?"

"Not the only ones that have fire," He reminded me. "Remember the matches? And besides, I think we'll need allies in the next few weeks to come. We could do a lot worse than sharing information with our neighbors and bringing them to our side."

Unless they use it against us, I thought uncharitably. I glanced over at the waiting duo, and Lana had her hand to her eyes, shielding them from the sun. She gave me a cheerful smile and I racked my brain, trying to remember what I'd been told about her. "What was her job again?"

Dean thought for a moment, then snapped his fingers. "Camp counselor. And I think I remember someone said that Will was a teacher."

"I guess they sound okay," I said, caving in. "I just worry that someone's going to mess this up for us when we've got things going so well."

Dean gave me a greasy hug, rubbing my arm. "Don't you worry about a thing." His hot, oiled skin slid against mine as he pulled me close. "I'll handle them."

To my vast shame, it felt marvelous to have Dean hold me close to him, feeling the sun-warmed skin against my own. The urge to sink against him was consuming. Lana was giving us an interested look, and too late, I remembered that we were supposed to be at each other's throats. I jerked away and followed Dean back over to Team Nine, trying to remain as nonchalant as possible, despite Lana's gloating grin.

"Fire for food sounds like a good deal to me," Dean said, stepping forward. Lana clapped her hands happily, and Will burst into a smile, and I realized just how much they'd needed fire. They were probably desperate for something to drink that didn't come out of a coconut.

Will handed the fruit over to Dean, who handed me a banana. I immediately began to peel it and eat it—the fruit inside was a little green and hard, but it was still one of the best things I'd eaten in a long time. I noticed Dean was eating his as well, and we made no pretense of trying to have a conversation as we scarfed the food down.

When I'd eaten the last bites of the banana and sighed, I pondered what to do with the peel. Maybe we could boil something in it later. Or... something.

"Fire?" Lana said expectantly.

Dean glanced over at me and nodded. He put his arm around Will's shoulders and gestured at the heavy thick of palms in the distance. "Why don't I have Will show me where the food is, and you show Lana the fire?"

I nodded and we split up, the girls heading back to our camp while the guys tromped into the heavy underbrush. Lana gave me a scrutinizing look as soon as they were out of sight. "So how are things with Dean?"

"Fine," I said slowly, not sure how much to reveal or how much she'd already guessed. "How are things with Will?"

"Very platonic," she said with a faint half-smile. "He's gay."

"Oh." I wasn't sure how to take that. Will was the only black man on the show, well-built and utterly gorgeous to look at. "So I guess you two aren't an item?"

Lana snorted, the sound overloud out of the petite asian woman. "He's been talking about your partner, Dean, for days now. No, I'm afraid that boy likes dick."

I laughed at that. "Well, Dean's the biggest dick on this island, so he came to the right place."

She grinned but the shrewd look returned. "Really? You two seemed cozy earlier. I noticed you were holding back in the reward challenge, too."

She had noticed all of that? Crap, Lana was far more observant than I liked. "I thought it might be a little obvious if we placed in first."

"It's a genius plan," Lana admitted. "When I saw you hesitating with that puzzle and then yelling at Dean, I thought you were pretty smart."

"I'd really appreciate it if you didn't say anything to anyone else," I said hesitantly. That she'd pegged both Dean and I so fast made me nervous.

"Say anything?" Her face broadened into a smile, and I realized for the millionth time how beautiful every single woman on this island was. "I'm not going to say a thing. I think the four of us would work better as allies."

I squatted next to the fire, poking the giant log we'd thrown over it before the challenge to keep it smoldering. Sure enough, the flames had died down but the coals at the bottom were still red. It wouldn't take much to get them hot again. "How are you going to carry this back?"

"Good question," Lana said. "I don't think we thought that far ahead.

We were just desperate enough to try anything.

I held out our boiling pot. "Dean and I haven't had a chance to use this yet. We can put some coals into this to carry over to your camp."

"That sounds good," she said, and Lana paced around our small camp, as if taking notes. "Your shelter is amazing," she gushed, leaning over it and examining where I'd woven the palm leaves together. "How did you get everything to hold together? I tried to build something but it fell apart the first night because of the wind."

I gestured at the shelter and tried not to feel too smug. "I used my string bikini to hold it together."

Lana gave me a startled look, then laughed again. "They are a little revealing," she agreed, though I noticed she was currently wearing hers. "And a blanket, too. Nice. Will got fish-hooks and I have some spices. What did you get?"

"I…" Oh lord, I really didn't want to tell her about my peanut butter. "I got a jar of some sort of food, but I dropped it in the water before I even hit shore," I said, making up the lie as I went along. "Pretty disappointing."

She made sympathetic noises. "I'll bet."

Once she'd finished the water, we filled the pot up with hot coals and carried it down the beach to their campsite, adding tinder to keep the fire going. Team Nine's beach was situated a mile away or so and across a small inlet. Not too long, really. A quick check out of their camp revealed what I'd suspected—their camp really sucked. No fire pit, no shelter, nothing. With Lana's help, I set out to creating a new fire for them, building the wood into a small pyramid and sending Lana to get tinder and other bits.

Dean and Will returned while we were building the fire, their arms full of fruit, and discussed where they'd found the fruit and the best places to find more. They seemed friendly enough, and when Will showed Dean the hooks, the men were determined to try and catch a fish. They spent most of the afternoon in the water while I helped Lana try and build a shelter similar to ours, though slightly bigger.

"It's not as cozy as yours, but I don't want to sleep snuggled up to Will unless it's cold," she said with a teasing note in her voice.

My throat froze at that. I wanted to point out that I'd originally built my shelter for me alone, but then that would reveal that the dislike Dean and I had affected wasn't always pretend. So I changed topics. "Do you want to tear strips from your shirt to lash the frame together or should we use your bikini too?"

Lana wanted to keep her bikini, so we tore a few small strips from the bottom of the hem of her shirt that had been provided, and set about building the rest of the shelter. By the time the sun was going down, we had a decent shelter built, the fire was crackling and merry, and there was freshly boiled water, coconut, and the men had even managed to catch two tiny fish, which were split four ways. There was a ton of merry conversation over the meager dinner, about Lana's overbearing Filipino parents, my job as a book reviewer, and laughing over how bad Dean and I had seemed the first day of challenges.

And when Lana brought up the alliance again, it didn't seem like such a bad idea. We agreed, all four of us placing our hands atop one another.

"To the end," Lana said, her cat-eyes gleaming in the darkness. "Final four."

"Final four," Dean, Will and I agreed.

Chapter Seven

You know, on day one, I wanted to be here with any woman but Abby. Now, I can't see any one but her.
—Dean Woodall, Day 6

"ARE WE SURE THAT WAS THE WISEST DECISION?" I ASKED DEAN AS WE walked back to our camp on the far end of the beach, our bellies (relatively) full and tired after a long day. The sun was down and the night air was getting chilly, which put the kibosh on our impromptu luau. I carried our cook pot in my arms again, a few coals flickering with fire at the bottom so we could rebuild our own. Dean walked beside me, his tall form shadowing my own, and we chatted as we headed back to our own camp. "I mean," I said, "I like Lana and Will but I still think they're playing the game to win on their own, and not win for us."

"They're not," Dean agreed with me. "But as long as we go in aware of that, I think we'll be fine. And we stand a better chance of making it to the end if we're four-strong instead of just two. They'll have our back and we'll have theirs…at least until we get closer to the end." On the moonlit beach, he looked over at me and grinned. "It's pretty smart, really. No one will think anyone is stupid enough to ally with us."

"We do seem to be a bad bet at the moment," I teased, glancing over at him and feeling that curious body flush when he looked my way. I resisted the urge to smile at him, knowing that it would come out goofy and wrong, and oh-so-obvious as to how I was feeling. Heck, I felt like I was wearing my emotions on my chest as boldly as I wore my name.

I had a thing for my partner.

I had no clue how that had happened, either. One day I was throwing paint on him for yelling at me, and the next I could think about nothing else but rubbing more bug lotion on his rock-hard muscles. Just a physical attraction, I told myself. Dean was by far the most attractive man on the island—tall, muscular, a beautiful smile, intelligent—but it could have also had something to do with the fact that he was the *only* man on the island, so to speak. At any rate, I was pretty sure it was one-sided, so the best thing to do would be to nip it in the bud. After all, there were a dozen hot women on this island, especially Lana. She was gorgeous and delicate, and filled out her string bikini in ways that would have been embarrassing on me.

"Something on your mind?" Dean said as we stepped back into our own small camp, and I knelt next to the now-out fire to dump the red-hot coals. "You seem quiet."

"Just tired," I said, trying to keep a cheerful note in my voice.

Before I even asked, Dean was handing me tinder and dried leaves to stoke up the fire, and his fingers were brushing mine. The simple action made my stomach flutter, and to my embarrassment, my nipples went hard.

"Cold?" Dean asked.

I grew even more flustered. Was he looking at my breasts? I turned away from the fire on the pretense of gathering more wood. "A little." My voice sounded strained. "They didn't leave us much to wear," I felt like I had to explain.

"Mmm," Dean said, staring at the fire as I tossed more bits and small pieces of wood onto it to build it into a decent flame. "Can't say I'm complaining."

I had to laugh at that, relaxing a little. Dean was just being Dean, and I was making myself crazy over nothing. "Yeah, well, you're not the one with your butt hanging out of a swimsuit the size of a hanky, either."

"Think I should complain to Chip that if the production crew is truly equal opportunity, they'd put us in Speedos?"

Now that would be a sight. "You'd probably have an island revolt from the other guys," I said, standing and brushing the sand off of my legs. "No straight man in his right mind would wear one of those things and expect to keep his pride intact. Now help me get some of this wood." I chuckled at the mental image and moved over to the far side of camp for a big, heavy log. We kept one or two of them nearby to bank the fire, and I thought it might be good to do before morning, so we could cook some of our rice bright and early.

"So you don't like Speedos, huh?"

"It's not that I don't like them," I called back, dragging the log forward. "But look at professional swimmers. It's hard to look straight in a Speedo, Dean. I think any guy that decides to shave his body, oil up and put on the equivalent of a man thong...well, I think he's looking to impress other guys, if you know what I mean."

"I do," he said in a weird voice.

I turned back to the fire and Dean had an odd look on his face. "Something the matter?"

He glanced back at me, and then stood, as if trying to shake it off. "No, I'm good. Ready to hit the sack?"

"Ready," I said. With his help, we lay the heavy log over the fire and banked it for the evening. Dean picked up his blanket and shook it out, sending a spray of sand into the wind.

I glanced over at the small shelter at the edge of our camp, a safe distance away from the fire pit. We'd spent all day at Lana and Will's camp, helping them build their shelter and fishing. Now, Lana and Will had a decent place to sleep and my partner didn't. It somehow didn't seem very fair. I realized Dean came to the same conclusion as he looked over at the snug shelter, and then began scanning the ground for a decent place to lay his blanket.

"We can both fit in there," I blurted, surprising even myself. "I'm sure we can both fit."

He seemed equally surprised at the offer. "Are you sure? It looks like it will only fit one person."

Well, of course it looked like that. I had built it for one person. But I was irritated that now I felt like an asshole for being so petty as to build a shelter for one in the first place. "We can both fit and share the blanket. Come on." When he hesitated a moment more, I added, "I don't bite, but the sand-fleas do. So either sleep out there and be miserable or crawl into bed with me, okay?"

He gestured at the small shelter. "After you, then."

I knelt and crawled into the small shelter, suspecting that Dean was going to either change his mind or push the entire rickety thing down on me. Something. And to be honest, I totally wouldn't blame him for doing it, either.

To my surprise, his head popped into the small shelter a moment later, his broad shoulders barely clearing the tiny A-frame. Dean paused a moment, looking down at the shelter, no more than two (maybe two and a half) feet wide. "Damn, this is small."

"Cozy," I agreed, feeling a little ashamed.

"You'd better lay out so I can crawl over you, or I don't think I'm going to be able to work my way in."

I nodded and did so, sliding down over the palm leaves that made my bedding. My skin was still slightly oily from the latest batch of the lotion, and I actually slid surprisingly easy. "We're all greased up, so it shouldn't be a problem getting in," I joked, then wished desperately that I could see his face in the darkness. But to make room for him, I turned on my side and faced the frame, trying to suck in and hold my body still enough that he could get in next to me.

It was…interesting, trying to squeeze another full-sized human being in my tiny shelter. I felt Dean's big body, all arms and legs and hard chest, and it became painfully obvious that there wasn't room for both of us to lay comfortably. His skin was touching mine no matter what he did, hot and slightly moist from the lotion. His slick skin slid against my back, his legs brushing up against my own as he twisted, trying to get comfortable.

After a moment, Dean swore, the sound close to my ear. "This isn't working."

I wanted to turn over in the shelter but I was afraid of conking him in the nose. "Why isn't it working?" His body constantly touched mine here and there, and every time it did, Dean backed away again. I kept myself poker-stiff, trying not to flail about and make it worse in my efforts to help him.

"Because," he began, shifting again. "I keep…touching you…no matter what I do. There's not enough room for us to both be in here and not touch." His breath exploded in a frustrated burst.

Oh, awkward. He didn't want to touch me? "Look, I'm not going to freak out if you happen to touch me the entire night. I'll feel a lot worse if I wake up and you're covered in sand, all right?" I reached over and tapped his arm, trying to indicate that he should lay down. "Just pretend I'm your girlfriend and we can spoon," I joked.

I needed to learn to shut my big mouth. No sooner did I say that, his hand slid over my waist, causing shockwaves to jitter through my body. His big body nestled next to mine, pulling me close in the most intimate embrace that I'd ever had. His legs were pressed to the backs of my legs, his cock nestled hard against my ass, his back plastered to my own. I almost complained, but it felt too nice to complain. And the man radiated heat. I liked being snuggled up to him a bit too much.

"That's nice," Dean said in a low voice. "Much better." I felt my hair move slightly, and could have sworn he inhaled.

Sniffing my hair? Surely not. I probably stank of eucalyptus and coconut and sea salt.

There was still a little bit of sand stuck to our skin, obvious with our bodies rubbed together, but strangely enough, I didn't mind it. And when Dean pulled the blanket over the two of us and then settled his arm back against my belly—under the blanket—I didn't say a thing. I only shifted so my head was pillowed on my bent arm, and tried to go to sleep.

'Tried' being the operative word, of course. Despite the exhaustion of living on the beach and eating almost nothing all day long, my entire body seemed to vibrate from within, and I was constantly aware of Dean's hand splayed on my stomach, pressing my slick body against his. Our bodies locked together, heated flesh against heated flesh, the only thing separating us being two tiny swimsuits. Part of me hoped that he would move his hand lower, or rub his hard cock against my ass a bit more and let me know that he was interested. Nip my shoulder. Something. Anything.

But he lay as quiet as me, and after an eternity of hoping, I fell asleep.

THE NEXT FEW DAYS FELL INTO A PREDICTABLE PATTERN. EACH MORNING we would wake up, clean up camp and stoke the fire, and cook breakfast. We'd work on improving our camp in the morning, and wander over to visit with Lana and Will in the afternoon. When dark hit, we headed back and curled up in our tiny bungalow, together, bodies pressed tight against each other.

It was playing hell with my self-confidence, too. Every day, it seemed that we shared an electrically-charged moment or two. Our fingers would touch and our eyes would lock. He'd spend a moment too long rubbing lotion onto my back. I'd watch him a bit too long as he arose from the ocean, glistening with sea water. The way his mouth would crook up on one side when he smiled down at me. The feel of his hips pressed up against my own at night.

It was making me so incredibly, unbelievably horny. And the man was completely uninterested. If I was sending signals, he wasn't receiving them. If I smiled at him, he turned away. If I pulled him a little bit closer at night, he snored. It was the uncertainty that held me back from making a full-on move. I was the least attractive woman on the island, sure, but I wasn't a troll either. How would he react if I flung myself at him? Would he just take what was offered and not think twice about it (which would be bad) or would he recoil in disgust (which would be very bad)? Even worse, how would it change our team dynamic? We were comfortable around each other now, and working smoothly as a team.

Smoothly enough that no one suspected our Honeymooners-like display was a total put-on. At each challenge, we made sure to bicker and shove at each other. I gave him open-handed slaps on his arm to convey my disgust, and he settled for withering scorn. In the four challenges in the past week—three immunity, one reward—we'd managed to carefully place just near the end. Lana had suggested that we purposefully lose the next reward challenge to throw people off, and so when it came to another swimming race, I was the one that swam. We lost by a mile, and Dean had pitched a fit on the beach that had sent camera-men flurrying about us and I rubbed my eyes so much after swimming in the salty ocean that I didn't have to fake the trickles that leaked from my eyes, especially when Lana and Will walked away with a big plate of peanut butter and chocolate that they devoured in front of everyone else. Back at camp, Dean had given me a comforting, friendly hug and tousled my hair. Like a kid.

That had depressed me far worse than losing the chocolate.

We'd squeaked out of landing in the bottom two spots in all of the immunity challenges, though we'd managed to perform poorly enough that we still looked incompetent. The next three teams that went home were the 'Mareen Biologest'—which made me smile widely—one of the swimsuit models, and Jody the Intern.

Judging by the information I'd been given prior to joining the show, we had three more group eliminations to go through before we merged as one big happy tribe. Dean and I kept track of the days by hash-marks on a tree, and we'd been out here for a little over two weeks. Incredible, that. My body was tanned and a good deal leaner than when I'd first landed on the island, my hair was a tangled mess that I wore in a thick braid just to keep it off my head, and my clothes were a briny mess that smelled like salt water.

I supposed it was just as well that Dean wasn't interested in me, I mourned as I picked rice kernels out of my breakfast bowl (made from a coconut half) and licked them off of my fingers. I didn't exactly look fresh-faced. I looked like I'd been stranded on a deserted island.

"Challenge today," Dean said as he opened our red mailbox and pulled out the message. Normally our messages were fairly straightforward, tied in a roll with a piece of twine to hold it shut. Once we'd gotten one written on the back of a coconut, and the challenge was coconut bowling (which we'd done terribly at, and not on purpose). This message was a square of parchment with long green grasses hanging off the edge, almost like a, well, like a grass skirt. It shivered and slithered when Dean shook the message, and I stood up and moved to his side to read over his shoulder.

As I did so, my breasts brushed against his arm and he glanced over at me in surprise.

"Sorry," I said in a meek voice and took a step backward, wishing he wouldn't look so darn surprised when I did that. It made me apologize. I didn't want to apologize to him—I wanted to grab his shoulders and climb all over him.

It was so very wrong.

Ignoring my apology, Dean handed the letter over to me and I began to read it aloud. "Today's challenge is a special one. You're guaranteed to have some fun. Pack your bags and pack your things. Who knows what tomorrow brings?" I flipped it over, just to check if anything was written on the back, and then frowned and handed it back to Dean. "That tells us nothing."

"Something's up," he said, shaking his head. "They wouldn't want us to bring our things unless they plan on doing some sort of switch-up."

My stomach dropped. "A switch-up? You mean, like changing partners?" That ruined everything. Oh no—what if I was stuck with someone like

Leon or Olaf the biker? I'd be screwed. Worse yet, Dean would be paired up with some cute little hottie and he'd forget all about me and my unrequited lust that he was determined to ignore.

Dean gave me a scrutinizing look. "Do you want to stay together?"

What? Why was he asking that? How was I supposed to respond to that? Or was he just taking the easy way out? Of course—it struck me at that moment. He probably wanted a more athletic partner. Someone a bit more pleasant than me. Someone cute and pretty and as athletic as, say, Lana. "Maybe."

His mouth crooked on one side. "Don't sound so excited at the prospect."

I was just being cautious. After all, leaping onto him and screaming, "Dean, I want to have your babies" seemed a little extreme, especially given that he'd never wanted to be paired with me in the first place. So I said, "Well, whatever happens, the four of us are going to stick together to the end, right?"

His mouth twisted slightly, his smile faint. "Right. The odds are in our favor if we work together, no matter who is on our team."

"Maybe it's for the best that we split up," I ventured slowly. "So we can influence our other partners." It sounded purely logical. It made me want to throw up. "After all, it's not like we wanted to be paired together in the first place."

His half-smile turned cold. "No, you got that right. We're in this for the money."

Ouch. That hurt a little more than I'd thought, hearing it come from his mouth. *We're in this for the money, and you're a lousy partner.* He might as well have spoken the rest of it out loud.

This felt ludicrous and hurtful. We should have been working together, trying to formulate some sort of plan. Figuring out how to stick together despite any sort of switch-up. Instead, here I was telling him it was for the best that we split up, and he was agreeing with me. My cynical heart that had been throbbing so hard in his presence felt crushed.

"We'd better get going," Dean said, crossing camp to grab his bag. "Boat'll be here soon."

I retrieved my pack out of the small shelter and felt the heavy weight of the peanut butter inside it. We'd been extremely stingy with it so far, taking small nibbles only before challenges. I remembered the scene with the first taste of peanut butter, how Dean's mouth had licked my fingers clean and

I'd stared at him, dumbfounded, as my pulse beat loudly in my ears.

And with that memory in my mind, I opened the can and dug a finger into the peanut butter one more time, and offered it to him. "Energy for the challenge?"

He glanced at me, and at my finger. I hadn't offered to 'feed' him the peanut butter since the first time, when he'd automatically reached out and taken me into his mouth. I could tell that he was thinking about that too. After a moment's pause, he nodded at the can. "I'll get my own."

I shrugged as if that didn't bother me, and put my finger in my own mouth, licking it clean and trying not to show how hurt I truly was at his refusal.

After all, this was a game. He was playing for two million dollars, and so was I. Of course he wasn't going to get romantic—especially with someone like me, so clearly not one of the other supermodel Playboy bunny types. I was far too normal for a god like Dean.

I continued sucking on my finger, sighing. Perhaps a new partner would be the best thing.

Chapter Eight

I think Abby hates me. Why else would she be so
determined to get away from me?
—Dean Woodall, Day 15

THE TEAMS FILED ONTO THE CHALLENGE BEACH, APPREHENSIVE. Bags were slung over shoulders, and I scrutinized the rest of the contestants for a moment. Everyone always seemed to look different after a few more days on the island, and today was no exception. Everyone was browner, their clothes dirtier. Shanna—the Playboy Bunny—had a very deep tan, but her legs were thin as twigs, and her implants stood out like boulders in her too-skinny frame. She looked like she needed a sandwich, and she wasn't the only one. Lana was starting to become wraith-thin, though still lovely. The other men were starting to grow extremely thin as well, losing their bulk. For once, I thanked the extra fifteen pounds I never seemed to shake. Lucky me.

I glanced out over the water, checking for challenge markers of any sort. Nothing. Interesting. Ahead, Chip stood atop a tall platform decorated with the Endurance Island logo. Eight booths were lined up facing him, but from the contestant angle, we couldn't see what was behind each booth, as they were covered with filmy white coverings that blocked the eye.

Normally, everything was color coded and numbered to match up with our teams—Team Eleven always had purple markers, for example. Today, though, there was nothing to mark each of the items as ours. I began to have a funny prickle in my stomach, and suspected that Dean was right.

This was a switch-up of some sort.

Chip greeted the teams as we entered, and I could tell by the expressions on the faces of the others that they were equally wary of this unusual set-up. The host raised his hand. "I need all the men to go and stand in a row on the red mat off to the side."

As a one, we all turned to look at the red mat. It was a long, single row off to the side with a bench behind it. That the men were moving over only gave me a bad feeling.

All around us, the other contestants were hugging their partners goodbye and separating. Dean turned and looked at me, and before he could say something or pretend to pick a fight, I reached out and gave him an awkward handsqueeze. For some reason, I really wanted to touch him before we got separated for good. He seemed a little surprised at my spontaneous gesture and did not hug me back, but looked as if he wanted to say something. The moment was broken too fast, though, and Dean moved away with the other male contestants, sitting in the midst of them like a king with his subjects.

"Ladies, if you'll move toward one of the booths here, but do not remove the coverings until I instruct so."

We moved forward, picking our way across the sand toward the covered booths. The camera-men zoomed in on the outskirts, hovering nearby to catch a glimpse of our faces at the big reveal. Chip seemed in his element, wearing a battered straw hat and beaming down at us, hands on his hips. "Today is a very important day for the ladies of Endurance Island," he began, launching into his host spiel. "On day one, the men chose their partners in a schoolyard pick. Today, however, Day Fifteen is Sadie Hawkins day. The ladies will fight for first place and the right to choose their partners."

Around me, the women clapped and showed enthusiasm, high-fiving each other. I crossed my arms over my chest and glanced down at Lana. At least I wasn't alone in my lack of enthusiasm. Lana's plans were ruined too, and she looked twice as annoyed as me.

"Today's challenge involves…fire!" Chip moved forward and leaned off of his platform, yanking the covering off of the nearest booth, displaying it to us. The booth was set up with a wide table, wood stacked underneath a small painted stool. Tufts of tinder were stuck in a decorated box, and small sticks and bits of kindling in a second box. On the table itself were a small knife and a flint. Across the table was a rope, which seemed to be attached to a pulley system and a big flag in front of the booth itself.

Chip pointed at each of the items and began to explain the rules to us. "The object of this competition is to build your fire high enough and hot enough to burn through the cord. When the cord snaps, this will raise your flag. The first flag to raise will win the challenge, get first pick of partners and the special bonus envelope." He held up a bright red square of paper in his hand. "The rest of the contestants will pick in the order that they finish. If you finish making your fire last, you pick last. Everyone understand?"

We moved forward to the booths we selected. I chose one in pale green, on the end of the contestants. I wouldn't be able to see how the others were doing, and that would probably be for the best, since it would just make me nervous. But this was a contest I could do well in. I knew how to make fire. I could do this.

But who would I pick if Dean didn't want to be my partner any longer?

I sat down on the shiny lacquered wooden stool and immediately stood up again. The stool was still wet with prop paint, and I wiped it off the back of my thighs in disgust. How cheap was the set? Ugh. I picked up the knife and flint and kicked the stool aside. I'd worked with flint to start a fire in my survival course. I could do this.

"Contestants ready?" Chip called, and I tensed over my table, thoughts racing. "Go!"

I grabbed a handful of tinder and then doubled it, making a huge mountain of it on my table. Tinder would burn fast and burn high, and I just needed to figure out how to get it to burn high enough to hit the rope that was at eye-level. I grabbed my flint and knife again, and scraped the edge of the blade against the flint. Nothing. I probably needed to strike fast and strike hard. With that in mind, I banged the two together and produced a tiny spark, but not enough to light my fluffy tinder-pile. I banged again, slicing the edges of my finger in the process, but the spark was bigger.

It took four more bangs (and subsequent cuts on my fingers) before I managed to get a spark to land in the fluff-pile. As soon as I saw a curl of smoke, I bent over and cupped the mound in my hands, blowing on it until smoke began to pour out.

"Someone's got a flame," Chip called over my head, and I hoped to God he was talking about me. I didn't dare look up, just continuing to blow on the tinder-puff until the flames were licking and I could hold it no longer. Then, I threw the entire box of tinder on top of my table, and added the kindling sticks, waiting for the entire table to go up.

It did, and pretty soon I had a low mass of flames on my table—the key element being 'low'. For some reason, my fire wasn't burning very high and my stuff was burning up entirely too fast, and I was nowhere near my string. Frustrated, I stared down at the wood underneath my table, trying to find small, dry logs to build my fire quickly. I picked up one, then two, but it was a slow lick, and it wouldn't get me to where I wanted. I needed to win, and fast.

"We have three…four…five fires going," Chip called behind me, as I fed the final scrapings of my tinder-box contents to my fire, adding the last of the small sticks to it. My larger logs still hadn't caught, and I began to get nervous and desperate. Could I burn something else? Was that against the rules?

I turned back to the host for a moment, feeding more logs at the edges of my fire to push it in. "What can we burn?" I cried at him. "Anything?" The fabric would be real handy right about now—I could drape one edge of it over the rope…

"Anything under the table," he called back at me, dashing my hopes. The fabric lay behind me, nowhere close to my table.

What was flammable? My shirt? No—it was the only T-shirt I had while I was out here, and I wasn't about to burn it. I rocked on my stool, thinking hard.

Wait, my stool. I stood up, jerking to my feet, and grabbed it. It was painted with a thick, glossy coat of paint, the exact same color as my light-green booth. It still gleamed wet and when my hand touched it, it was sticky. The paint wasn't dry. Wasn't paint flammable? I grabbed it, flipped it upside down, and held it over the licking flames.

"What are you doing?" Chip yelled at me from behind the dais, and immediately the camera-man nearby zoomed in to my booth.

"You said I could use anything under my table," I called, and a ripple of laughter emerged from the men's row in the distance.

I held the stool over the licking flames, hoping the wet, sloppy prop paint would catch on fire. The actual wood of the stool felt light and cheap to me—lighter than plywood—and I wouldn't be surprised if it burned faster than anything they'd given me in my woodpile. Sure enough, the bottom began to lick flames, and I set it down in the already burning-fire. The flames began to flicker and dance over the surface, turning green and blue as the paint burned off, and I stepped backward slightly, using my log to shove the rest of the burning crap on my table over the stool.

It was burning like a beacon, and I wondered at the cheapness of the props on the island. Heh. One of the legs began to burn and I angled it so it was touching my rope, and waited, glancing down the row at the others. Lana had noticed what I was doing and was using her stool as well, though with less success.

The fire was licking up the cheap legs of the stool and licking toward the rope already, and I watched as the other women glanced over at my fire and began to use theirs as well, stools thumping onto the tables right and left as women stood and tried to copy my success.

There was a snap, and my flag shot into the air. "Abby wins first place," Chip called out in a sour voice. Apparently he didn't like my bending of the rules. I didn't care. I clapped my hands and sucked in a deep breath, trying to calm the frantic beating of my heart. My god, I'd *won* something. It felt good.

One of the production assistants off-camera motioned for me to go and stand next to Chip, and I did so, waiting for the others to finish. I scanned the line of men remaining. I'd have first pick of partners, and they knew it. None of them were making eye contact with me, except Dean, who flashed a brilliant white smile in my direction that made my knees weak. So as not too seem too obvious, I looked up and down the row of men. Tattooed Leon was still there, and Olaf the biker. Will smiled at me, but it was uncertain and I knew he didn't want to be separated from Lana unless we were told we couldn't pick our old partners. I totally understood that, and gave him a small nod. The others I hadn't ran into very much—Shane, Chris, Jack, Riley.

Dean was so much better than them in every aspect. I thought of the tiny shelter back on our beach, and our bug repellent. Did I want to curl up with someone else in that shelter? Rub bug lotion all over their bodies? Have them lick peanut butter from my skin?

"Lana," Chip shouted in my ear. "Second place!" Then, "Ginger, third!"

Slowly, the rest of the women finished. Well, sort of. Both Heidi and a girl named Heather hadn't been able to create fire, so they were forced to draw straws, and Heather ended up with last pick. At last, Chip returned to me and I wiped my sweating palms on the edge of my shirt, nervous.

He held out the red envelope. "As first place, you receive this envelope. Open it and read aloud."

I took it from him with shaky fingers, unnerved at the fact that all eyes were completely fixed on me and my movements. There was a wax seal on one side, and I broke it with my thumbnail and flipped the letter open, reading aloud.

"As winner of this reward challenge, a choice must be made. Either get first pick of partners and increase your odds, or elect a day in the shade." As usual, the messages written by the staff were crappy and made no sense, so I turned to Chip for my answer.

"You have two choices, Abby. One, you can take first pick of the male contestants. Any of them that you want. This can give you a huge advantage over the others. Or," he said, and paused dramatically, "You can forego strategy and select the reward instead. If you select reward, you will be taken to a luxury spa and will spend the night there. You'll have food, showers, and a warm bed waiting for you. But the down-side is that you'll be forced to remain with your current partner, and will receive no strategic advantage."

No strategic advantage? It sounded like paradise to me—vacation, food, shower, *and* Dean? But what if I was the only one that wanted that? It occurred to me that I might be making Dean the most miserable person on earth if I kept him with me, and I quickly glanced out to him, looking for my answer in his face. As usual, he wore no expression, not giving away anything. That was no help. I had no idea if I was making the right choice or not. Panicked, I scanned the row of men one last time, trying to decide.

To hell with this.

I'd lived several days with angry Dean before. I could live with angry Dean again. Even if it did make my stomach knot at the thought of him being angry at me after the bonding we'd done. But, my decision made, I handed the red card back to Chip. "I want the food," I said.

"Of course," Shanna said down the line, her voice catty. Someone snickered next to her.

Chip seemed very surprised by my choice. "You're deciding to keep the same partner?" He said, as Dean rose to his feet in the distance and slung his back over his shoulders, the expressionless look still on his face. "After all the troubles the two of you have had for the past two weeks, what made you choose that?"

Uh oh, I had to explain myself. "I really just wanted the food and shower," I said in a bright voice, hoping that my bubble-headed lie sounded convincing. "Who wouldn't?"

Chip gave a fake chuckle and gestured in the distance. "If you'll go that way, you'll be taken to your reward."

With my bag clutched tightly in my hands, I trailed off of the small stage, back down to the ground. One of the production assistants was waiting nearby, ready to interview me about my win. Dean was in the distance, heading toward me, and I offered him a faint smile as he walked by. "Hi," I called, just before another production assistant grabbed him.

He turned and gave me a hard look. "We'll talk later."

That didn't bode well. I swallowed and nodded. If this was a show for the cameras, well…he certainly had me convinced.

While there were many tiny things I really disliked about the rules of Endurance Island, the worst had to be the 'no talking' rule on transportation. Since the show was all about filming every aspect of our day in the island setting, talking on the motorboats would interfere with that, so the simplest show rule was "No talking at all" during transport. Which was fine, normally, but as I sat in the helicopter with Dean next to me, our legs touching, it was hard to stick to the rule.

I wanted to find out if he was mad at me. If I'd made the wrong decision.

The helicopter dropped us off at a designated pad on a different island, and a woman was there to greet us and take our backpacks, since we weren't allowed to bring them on reward. She had the long, wavy hair and round face of the native Islanders, and was dressed in a colorful wrap dress and wore a flowered wreath. "Come," she gestured at us, her voice barely audible as the helicopter took off again, and I felt (rather than heard) the familiar camera-man moving into place to the side.

The woman led us up a long flagstone path to a small beach house with large windows. The heavily slanted roof and bushy palms surrounding it were supposed to give an air of privacy to the hut itself, but I could see the rest of the hotel in the distance, and it felt weird to be so close to civilization once more. Our escort led us up the stairs to the bungalow and opened the door, then gestured that we should enter. "Your food is waiting for you inside. Please ring the bell if you need anything," she said, then walked to the edge of the bungalow porch to demonstrate the bell. "I will come and assist you with anything you require. The helicopter will return in the morning to take you back to the beach."

"Thank you," I murmured, not looking at my partner. It sounded like it would be just the two of us. An anticipatory tingle skittered over my skin, but that was ridiculous.

Dean thanked her as well, and she moved down the steps and away, leaving us alone in the small island bungalow. Dean glanced at me.

My mouth dried at the expectant look he was giving me. He clearly wanted answers, and the only ones I could think of started with *I didn't want to be separated from you...* which just sounded desperate. I pushed past him into the cabin, looking around.

The smell of food hit like a brick, and my mouth began to water immediately. I followed it into the large living room area of the tiny house. The bungalow seemed to be built with a very open layout—one half of the entire house was the living room area, and a long, low table overflowed with food. Two pillows sat on either end of the table, I assumed, for us to sit on.

I dropped my bag in the doorway and went to check the rest of the bungalow. One small room was a bedroom, with two tiny twin beds separated by a wicker nightstand. Two fluffy bathrobes lay nearby, along with two colorful wraps for us to wear when we were done showering. The other room was an immense, almost palatial bathroom that I could have sworn was bigger than the bedroom. Decorated in tropical style, it consisted of a stone floor and massive dual showerheads, separated by a saloon door partition. His and hers showers. Cute.

Dean had drifted in behind me, and was staring at the bathroom with an impressed look on his face. "Pretty nice digs."

"Yep," I said, still feeling awkward, and brushed past him, out of the bathroom and into the living room, making a direct line toward the food. A pizza dripping with cheese and pepperoni still had steam rising from it, and with my mouth watering, I reached out to grab a slice...and stopped, appalled at the filth on my hand. Rings of dirt scored under my fingernails, and my tan was ringed with grime from living on the beach. Suddenly, I felt filthy as hell, and wiped my hand on my equally gritty shirt. Ugh.

Dean moved behind me, and his hand touched my shoulder. "Abby, I think we need to talk." His voice was serious and low, and distinctly not what I wanted to hear at the moment.

No, no. "I don't want to talk right now," I said, trying to brush past him. I didn't want to ruin the lovely mountain of food or the showers or anything with an argument or complaining about my lack of strategy. I just wanted to enjoy an evening of luxury.

"We need to talk," Dean insisted, following me as I pushed past him.

"I'm going to shower first," I said, not looking at him as I moved into the bedroom, scooped up the robe, and then crossed to the bathroom. "You're welcome to talk to me in there, but I'm filthy and I'm going to clean up before I touch any of that lovely food."

To my relief, he didn't follow me into the bathroom. I stepped into one of the stalls, the door swinging behind me, and began to strip out of my clothing. I didn't care if it got wet—hell, it needed to be cleaned worse than I did. I stepped out of the last of my bikini and tossed it in the corner of the shower, then turned the water on.

It blasted on my skin, hot and wet and just about the best thing ever. I gave a shuddery moan of delight and wet down my hair, leaning into the spray with intensity. God, it felt so amazing. Who would have thought a warm shower could feel so blissful after two weeks of no showers? I grabbed one of the small bottles of shampoo lining the wall and shampooed my thick, curly hair. Twice. The scent was coconut—something I was a little tired of—but I didn't care. It felt heavenly to get clean.

A round, lumpy sponge had been left for me, and I squirted it with body wash, frantically rubbing down my body. As I did, I heard the shower next to me turn on, and glanced over the swinging doors. Dean was in the other shower, and I could just make out his shoulders and hair as he soaped up. "Decided to shower?" I called out.

He slicked the water away from his face and glanced at me over the flimsy shower door. "Thought I'd wait for you."

I nodded and turned back to my frantic body scrubbing. Part of me supposed that I should have been weirded out by sharing a shower with a stranger, but Dean felt like anything but a stranger. Living together on a beach for two weeks had certainly stripped that aspect out of our relationship, and I figured he could see flashes of my naked body in the shower, and I pretty much didn't care. Though, if I had to admit it, I was curious to see him without his trunks.

I blushed at the thought and chided myself for it. We had to work together—professionally—at least until the tribes merged. I couldn't be sitting here, wondering how big his equipment was. We were friends. Theoretically. He might be mad at me for screwing his chances, and I might have been thinking about his package, but we were friends before today, and hopefully we would be again after the initial shockwaves settled down.

"So why did you pick me?" Dean said loudly, speaking over the water.

What was the best answer here? "Because they expected me not to," I called back.

"Trying to prove everyone wrong again, eh?"

I couldn't tell from the tone of his voice if he thought I was being funny, or what, so I said nothing, swiping the sponge over my neck and the tops of my shoulders. I couldn't quite reach my back, and it was bothering me.

"Abby?" Dean stepped forward, and I glanced over my shoulder at him. He was standing near the swinging doors, but his eyes were averted, not looking at my naked (and very vulnerable) body. For some reason, I found that…sweet. My heart melted. Even though he was irritated at me and I was standing here naked, he was averting his eyes, like a gentleman.

"Something like that," I said slowly. My back still felt oily and gross, and I took a step backward, keeping my back presented to him. "Can you wash my back while we talk?" I kept my eyes trained forward, stating without speaking that I wouldn't look at his naked body if he did. To keep my promise, I closed my eyes and bent my head, crossing my arms over my breasts and exposing my back.

After a moment's pause—and I had a horrible fear that he wouldn't do me the favor—I heard him step forward, and then a soapy sponge—his—brushed across my shoulders. He swiped in quick, functional, almost rough motions. Impersonal. "So that's why you picked me?" His voice was as neutral as his touch. "Just to fuck with the others?"

Food and showers help, I wanted to say, but I bit my tongue, remaining silent. Anything I said right now would come across as flippant, and I just wanted to concentrate on him touching me.

The sponge finished scrubbing my back, and it lifted and started over at my shoulders, moving in small, almost ticklish circles. Still washing me with soft, easy strokes.

"Abby?"

"What?" My voice grew shy, my skin prickling as my mind went wild with the thought of him standing naked behind me. This wasn't going to work. I should have sent him off with another team. I should have picked someone safe like Will. I should have—

"Are you going to stand there and tell me that's the only reason you picked me?" Dean said in a low, hoarse voice. The sponge lifted from my shoulders, and I felt nothing but the hot spray of water on my body, and Dean's intense presence behind me.

I dared to risk a glance over my shoulder, and found him standing close to me, very close. My entire body prickled with awareness, and my heart pounded. *Don't say anything*, I warned myself. *Don't say anything. He can't possibly be interested in you as a person. This is a game and he's just going to use you to win the money.*

But his fingers—not the sponge—rested along the dip of my spine, and I sucked in a breath, steeling myself. "Not the reason," I whispered. The air seemed charged with electricity and hope, and I froze, waiting for him to tell me if I was nuts. I squeezed my eyes shut, waiting.

Rough hands grabbed my shoulders and my eyes flew open as Dean whirled me around and grabbed me in his arms, and then his mouth was hot on mine, kissing me frantically. Devouring me. His lean, hard body pressed against mine, and I felt the thick erection against my stomach, even as he pressed our bodies closer together. My hands lifted, winding to his neck as my mouth pressed against his with equal fervor. His mouth nipped at mine and he sucked on my lower lip, making my breath gasp into my throat. Dean's hands pushed me against the slick tile wall, pressing me between him and the wall itself, a cage of flesh as his arms surrounded me. I whimpered a little at the sensation, swiping at his tongue with mine and digging my fingers into his hair. It was madness, this intensity between us, nothing but water and steam and frantically kissing mouths, as if a dam had burst and the water had washed away all inhibition and doubt.

"I thought you wanted a different partner," Dean breathed into my mouth, even as his hands slid up the sides of my breasts. I writhed against the wall, against his chest, my hands frantically moving from his hair to his shoulders, everywhere I could touch him.

"I didn't think you'd want to be with me," I said, averting my face with the pretense of pressing tiny bites along the strong line of his jaw. God, I loved his jaw. Two weeks worth of whiskers didn't detract from his beauty at all.

"That's fucking stupid," he said, grabbing my leg and hooking it over his hip. "I've been crazy about you ever since we got here and you glared at me like I was dirt. Couldn't figure you out." His mouth pressed against my neck, the words muffled, and his hand lifted my leg a little higher, his hips jutting forward until the full length of his erection pressed against my sex, and my breath escaped me in a shuddering gasp.

Well, that didn't leave much to the imagination. And the reality was so much better. And bigger. I moaned against him and bit his ear, frantic.

He groaned, bucking his hips against me again, his fingers sliding up to flick a wet nipple. "You sure you want this? Last chance to back away," he said, his thumb grazing my nipple, back and forth. "Look at me, Abby."

Almost shy—despite our frantic, desperate make-out session—I lifted my eyes to his, our faces sprayed by the water of the shower.

"Do you want this?" He repeated, and a slight swivel of his hips left nothing to the imagination as to what he was referring to. "If you tell me to stop now, I will."

His thumb hadn't stopped, though. It was still teasing the peak of my breast, the slick skin rubbing back and forth in a motion that sent shock-waves up and down my body. I wanted to reach down and bite his thumb, bite his mouth, devour him whole even as he pressed against me, his wet hair plastered to his skull.

"If you stop now, I'll never speak to you again," I said, and arched so my breast rubbed against his hand in a very deliberate fashion, the other peak brushing against his chest.

He pressed a hard, frantic kiss to my mouth and released my leg. "Wait here." With that, he cupped my face in his hands, kissed my mouth again—softly—and left me in the shower. Dean stepped out of the shower and into the bathroom, and as I watched and waited, my arms crossed over my breasts again, he dug through the drawers of toiletries. A small foil packet appeared a moment later, and he returned to my side, as if we'd never left off, grabbing me in the circle of his arms again and pushing me back against the slick wall. His free hand locked in mind, our fingers interlaced, and he slid our twined hands up the tile until my body was arched slightly, my breast tilted towards the air, and he bent over and took the peak in his mouth.

I cried out, my hips bucking slightly at that. "Dean!"

He bit lightly at the peak, then his hair brushed against my breast, and I heard the sound of the foil packet tearing. His hands moved away from mine for a moment—too long a moment—as he put on the condom. Then, one hand slid down my thigh, hooking my leg around his hip again, and his mouth devoured mine once more. Hard, fast, wet, his tongue thrust into my mouth. The cradle of my hips lay against his erection again, his hips circling and moving ever so slightly against my own spread legs.

"You ready, baby?" he whispered against my mouth, and I felt his hand tug at my other leg, the only thing supporting me other than the two immovable objects I was wedged between.

I wrapped my arms around his neck and kissed him back, biting at his lip. He growled low in his throat and lifted me off the ground, ever so slightly, my back sliding up the slippery wall. The head of his cock probed against me, and before I could suck in a breath, he slid me down on the hard length of it, spearing me and bracing me against his own hips.

My breath shuddered out of my throat, my arms clenching tight around his neck. Amazing. Holy God. His hands slid to my ass, and his hips moved slightly, as if settling me against him, and the slight motion made all the breath whisper out of my throat again.

He pressed an open-mouth kiss to my lips. "Feel good?"

All I could manage was a shuddery gasp, and I dug my fingernails into his shoulders. Dean rocked his hips slightly again, and the small motion made friction happen in just the right places, and I gave another weak gasp.

"Abby," he whispered against my mouth, thrusting slightly again, his fingers digging into my hips. "God, you are so fucking sexy." Again, a small thrust and wriggle, and the pulse of friction that shot through my body. My legs locked around his hips, and I squeezed my inner muscles the next time he thrust, and he moaned against my mouth as well.

The next thrust was harder, more forceful, more friction. The next, too, and his arms were cords of steel as they locked my hips against his, shoving me back against the wall, thrusting slightly. Those gentle, deep thrusts were undoing me more than anything I'd ever experienced before, and it wasn't long before my hips were bucking slightly against his own, increasing the friction, and I began to shudder, gasping as an orgasm ripped through me in slow, steady waves. The feeling intensified as he thrust into me again, rapidly, and I felt his strong body tremble against mine, a groan escaping his mouth as he pressed me against the wall so hard that I thought I'd sink through it. I clung to him, body slick and trembling as he finished his orgasm and slowly released my rubbery legs, sliding me back down to the ground and our bodies separating.

He wasn't done with me, though. His hands moved to my wet hair, brushing it off of my face and planting several more hot kisses on my dazed face. "I'm sorry—that didn't last as long as I wanted to." Dean's hands slid to my waist, a possessive gesture.

Was that him not at his best? His worst was better than my last boyfriend's 'best'. "Short is good," I said weakly. "The water's getting cold."

He pressed another possessive kiss on my mouth. "Next time we're doing it on the bed."

Next time? My mouth curved slightly at that…and then my stomach rumbled. He laughed, and I gave a small chuckle. "Can we eat our food first?" I said in a small, plaintive voice. "That pizza looked amazing."

We turned off the shower and his hand went to the small of my back, steering me back out of the bathroom in an intimately possessive gesture. The colorful sarongs were the only things we had to wear, so I wrapped up in one while Dean knotted the other at his waist, the fabric slinging low on his hips. Low enough to make me breathless. He caught my glance and the self-confident smile slid over his face. "There's more for you later, baby."

I rolled my eyes at his cocky, teasing voice, drying my hair with the towel and then discarding it on the floor. Dean moved ahead of me into the living room, where the food was laid out, and it took everything I had not to race past him to get to the food first. There would be plenty for both of us, and it was hard to quell the competitive edge to my starvation.

Dean moved to the far side of the table, but instead of sitting down, he grabbed his seat-pillow and dragged it over by mine, so we could sit together. He patted the pillow next to his. "Come, sit. We'll eat our way from one side of the table to the other."

Sounded good to me—I moved to sit next to him and curled up on my cushion, legs crossed. There was a bucket of ice and Corona nearby, and Dean pulled two beers out, twisting the cap off of mine with his bare hand, and then handing it to me. Quite the gentleman. I took a sip of the beer and closed my eyes. "Heaven."

I took another sip, washing the flavor in my mouth slowly, savoring it, and looked over to see Dean doing the same. Well, sort-of. His gulps were twice the size of my sips, but he had the same blissed-out expression. My stomach growled again, and the sight of all the amazing food was too much to wait any longer for—I grabbed one of the thick brown plates and handed him one, taking the other for myself, and began to load it up with food, tasting as we went. There were chicken wings with buffalo sauce, celery sticks with dip, potato chips, pretzels, pizza, hot dogs, chili, and just about everything you could imagine for a tailgate party. Except football, of course. I laughed as I accidentally spilled some of the chili on my fingers and Dean leaned over and licked it off my hand. "Do you think they're going with a theme here?" I asked.

He nodded, then took enormous bites out of the relish-covered hotdog in his hand. "They're going to see how sick they can make us," he said around bites.

I didn't care—I grinned and took a bite of the pizza, and gave a moan of delight at the taste. If I never ate again, I'd still die happy.

Dean glanced over at me and smiled, a boyish look. To my surprise, he reached over and grabbed my left hand as I reached for a beer, and examined it with great curiosity, his emphasis on my fingers. Then, he looked over at me, relieved. "Not married?"

He'd been looking for a wedding band. My heart skidded to a stop. "No," I whispered.

"Boyfriend?" He asked, trying to keep his voice light as he released my hand and reached for another beer. He didn't look me in the eyes.

"No boyfriend," I said in a small voice. The world crashed down around me, a little. Okay, a lot. "You?"

His mouth quirked. "No, no boyfriend."

I threw my napkin at him. "You know what I mean." Oh god, I couldn't breathe. I couldn't think—I couldn't see his hand behind that beer bottle—

"Nothing," he said, shaking his head. "Currently between ex-girlfriends."

My breath whooshed out of me in a relieved gulp, and I choked, coughing on the food in my mouth. Dean thumped me on the back. "You okay?"

When I regained my breath, I gave him a horrified look. "Dean, I just realized…we don't know each other." I knew that, and I still wanted to run into the other room with him and throw him down on the bed. How horrible was that? How wrong?

"I know you," he said, shaking his head. "You make a mean fire, you can't paint for shit, and you taste like peanut butter." Dean winked at me, and the mix of playfulness and lust on his face sent a bolt of desire straight through me again. "I know all about you."

"But you don't know me…really know me." My voice raised in a slight panic.

He handed me another beer, twisting the cap off and placing it in my hand as if I were helpless. Then, he thought for a moment, and clinked the neck of his beer against my own. "Then we get to know each other tonight." He smiled slowly. "And tomorrow. And the day after. And all the time we have left on this island. Baby, you and me have nothing but time."

The low, sexy way he said it made me blush, and I took another sip of beer, trying to quell my nervousness. Some women jumped into bed with strange men, lived life as a series of one-night stands. I did not. For me, sex didn't come without emotional attachments. *Stay calm*, I told myself. *Drink more beer. Everything's better with beer.*

"Why don't you ask me something, and I'll ask you something," Dean offered, munching on pretzels. We'd finished eating the majority of our meal—I imagined that his stomach hurt as much as mine with all the food we'd hastily crammed into it—but there was still the incessant need to snack, to stockpile carbs for when they disappeared again.

I grabbed a celery stick and swirled it in the dip, then bit down. "How old are you?"

"Twenty-eight. You?"

Not a bad age. "Twenty-six."

"Ever been married?"

"No, never," I said.

"Me either," Dean said, reaching for a celery stick of his own. "Came close once."

"Want to talk about it?"

He laughed. "Not tonight. Wouldn't do good to talk about my ex-girl-friend in front of my current one."

So I was his girlfriend? A silly trill shot through me at that, and I gave him a dopey smile. "I'm from DC. So where are you from?"

"Houston," he said, cocking his head to the side as he regarded me. "You sounded southern, I thought."

"I am," I amended. "I'm working in DC but I grew up in Amarillo."

"Texas, too?" Dean grinned. "But not my part of Texas. Next you'll be telling me that you're a Cowboys fan."

I shook my celery stick at him. "They are 'America's Team', you know." At his snort of outrage, I laughed and reached for another beer.

Football seemed to break the awkward dam between us, and we launched questions at each other that we'd been to self-absorbed to ask up to this point. Personal questions—like how many sisters Dean had (three), and how many pets I had (a cat). We moved to not-so personal stuff like sports and karaoke. We both loved the former and hated the latter. Both of us liked the same music, and we'd even hung out at the same bars in Austin during our college years.

At some point, we'd eaten a few bites of everything and had drank nearly all the beer. As we'd moved down the table, tasting food and chatting about random stuff—none of it game-related—our seating pillows slid closer and closer together, until at some point, I was leaning on Dean's corded arm as he fed me another pretzel stick. Or tried to, but I was yawning too hard.

"Sleepy?" he asked, shifting me to an upright position.

I nodded and tried to hide another yawn. "It's the beer. Always does that." I was sleepy and more than slightly woozy with the alcohol running through my starved system. How many beers had I drank? Five? Six? Dean had easily downed as many as me, though he seemed to be handling the effects well. I peered at him. "Does this mean we're going to get drunk and go make out again, now?"

Dean chuckled, getting to his feet and extending his hands to help me up. "I think one of us is already drunk."

I slid against him, my legs boneless, and laughed as he reached to catch me, dragging my body against his. His bare chest felt so hot and nice against my own flesh, and I immediately slid my hands from his neck and down his shoulders. Dean had to be the best looking man I'd ever slept with, with the broadest shoulders and the nicest tan, and that sly grin that did crazy things to my knees. I focused on his mouth and realized he was grinning even now, which probably explained why I was having difficulty standing. "Hi," I said breathlessly.

"Let's get you to bed," he said, looping his hand around my waist and making sure that my arm was anchored over his shoulders. I let him lead the way as he half-walked, half-dragged me to the bedroom as the room spun around me.

My stomach heaved uncomfortably.

"You okay?" Dean whispered. "You just got really pale."

"I don't feel so well," I said in a light voice, trying to push away from him.

To my surprise, Dean picked me up in his arms and carried me to the bathroom, setting me on the floor next to the toilet. My stomach spun and churned, and I moaned and sank to the floor next to it, laying my cheek against the cool white porcelain.

"Too much beer and too much weird food," Dean said, stroking my hair back as it fell in my face. "Are you going to be sick?"

I closed my eyes, as if that would help my stomach. "Don't know yet."

He walked away, and that simple act made my stomach churn a little more. The thought of me being sick made *him* ill.

I couldn't blame him. We'd just gotten clean after two weeks of filth. Still, it embarrassed me that I'd repulsed him, and I closed my eyes, laying still and praying for the vomit to stay down.

It did not.

Someone moved a minute or two later, and I opened my eyes to see Dean was back at my side, offering me a slice of bread and a glass of water. Surprised, I stared up at him as he held the bread out. "You need to eat and drink this." I groaned at the sight, but he insisted. "Hangover prevention food—trust me."

And he pushed the slice into my hand, and didn't budge until I began to take small bites of the bread. When I was done with the bread, he handed me the glass of water, and watched until I finished it as well.

"Thank you," I said in a small voice. I didn't know what to make of his thoughtful return. He could have left me on the floor and gone to sleep and I wouldn't have thought any worse of him, but this was…startling. And nice. "I feel better," I added.

"You'll be fine after you sleep it off," he told me, and helped me to my feet again. This time, we moved more slowly, with greater caution so as not to upset my stomach once more.

We moved back to the small bedroom, and I glanced at the two twin beds. A thin blanket covered each one, and the white pillows seemed inviting. I sat down on the edge of the closest one, and Dean helped me into the bed, pulling the covers over me. I tilted my head up to look at him and he gave me a quick kiss on the forehead, then moved to his bed.

Bed—for the first time in two weeks. So pleasant.

It turned out to be impossible to sleep in. The covers got hot within minutes, sticking to my skin and feeling smothering. The tiny bed was almost too soft, and I flailed back and forth in bed, miserable. It was like I was missing something, and it grated on me so much that it was physically impossible to sleep.

After I turned over for the hundredth time, Dean rolled over in his bed. "Can't sleep?"

"No," I said in a miserable voice. "There's something wrong with my bed."

"Too comfortable?"

I gave him a miserable laugh. "Maybe. Who would have thought?"

"You can come sleep with me." In the darkness, I heard him pat his bed. "Just like back at camp. Actually, the camp bed is probably smaller."

He had a point. I hesitated for a moment, wondering if he'd think I was too forward if I leapt back into bed with him, and then decided that I didn't care. I slipped out of my bed and over to his, where he held the covers open for me. Turning my back to him, I slid into bed next to Dean, so we could spoon as we always did on the island.

My backside nestled against his, and his arm went around my waist as always, and he pulled the covers over me. "See, plenty of room."

Strangely enough, it did feel roomy compared to our little shelter, and I snuggled down next to him, my body fitting against his comfortable, familiar molding. "Thank you, Dean." And though it was hot under the covers within moments, his skin warm against my own, neither one of us moved, and I fell asleep within moments, his hand splayed low on my stomach.

Chapter Nine

Holy crap. I totally did not mean for that to happen. But at the same time…I don't regret it. Not in the slightest.
—Dean Woodall, Day 16

I WOKE UP TO THE DELICIOUS FEELING OF A BROAD CHEST AGAINST MY back, an arm locked around my waist, and a pillow under my head. In fact, it felt so wonderful I didn't want to open my eyes.

"I can tell you're awake," Dean whispered against the back of my head. "You're twitching."

With a groan, I flipped over and burrowed against his chest, trying to hide from the sunny, too-bright world. "If I wake up, that means we have to go back."

He laughed at that, and I felt the rumbles in his chest through my own body. Dean's hand had slid to my hip, where my sarong had bunched up high on my legs. He was rubbing the exposed skin there with slow, smooth circles, as if he couldn't resist touching me. My face grew hot as I recalled—whoever had left us the sarongs had not left us matching underwear.

But I didn't feel the urge to move, or to push Dean's hands away. I remembered the shower last night, and our explosive, frantic sex. That had been the most singularly awesome sexual experience I'd ever had, but

I wasn't sure how to initiate it again. My eyes slid open and all I could see was the lean, darkly tanned muscles of Dean's torso. He'd lost so much weight in two weeks that his six-pack was etched and defined, and some of the bulk of his body was gone. Not that it made him unattractive—not by a long shot.

His breath fanned slowly on my hair, my head tucked under his chin. His hand continued to move in the soft, stroking motion, sliding up and down the swell of my hip and buttock. I looked down at my bare hip, the blankets around our thighs, and gave a small sigh at the sight. "I'm getting bony."

"You're beautiful. Always have been."

My breath caught in my throat at that, warmth flooding through me, and I suddenly wanted him very much again. With gentle fingers, I slid my hand out from where it was tucked against my own body and brushed the taut skin over his abdomen. Inviting him.

Dean's mouth pressed against my forehead, and he gave me a soft kiss, his lips grazing my hairline before moving lower. His fingers that had been stroking my hip grew possessive, clenching me toward him, and my eyes flew to his when a hot, naked erection prodded my stomach through the thin sarong. "You're not dressed?"

He shook his head down at me, a slow, sensuous smile curving his mouth. "You're hardly dressed yourself." As if to prove this point, his hand slid up my bare hip, pressing the loose sarong further up my body, exposing my backside. His hand skimmed the curve of my lower back, exploring. "No panties," he said, leaning in to press another gentle kiss on my face, this time on my eyebrow.

It seemed we'd decided to have a slow, languid mutual exploration of bodies, and I was certainly game for that. My hand slid across his abdomen to his side, to the ridge of hard muscle where his thigh met his groin. Only men in the most incredible shape seemed to have that sort of muscle ridge, and I'd never seen one before on anyone I'd slept with. I was fascinated with his body. "You must work out a lot back home," I whispered, skimming the fascinating part of his body with my fingernail.

He chuckled at that, burying his face into my hair. "I guess you could say that," he said, his voice muffled. Before I could ask what was so funny, he kissed my face again, pressing small, light kisses on my cheekbone, my ear, my nose, my chin, before moving to my lips and continuing the same

light, fluttery presses that made me tremble. I lay still under his ministra-
tions for several long minutes as he gently kissed every inch of my face, his
hand kneading my backside and making my entire body quiver.

When I could stand being still no longer, I lifted my leg and wrapped it
around his hips, pulling his body closer to mine. I sought his mouth with
my own, my hands moving to his hair and wrapping in the tousled sleepy
cowlicks. Dean made a low, hungry noise in the back of his throat and his
tongue met mine in a quick plunge. We kissed, a melding of tongues and
lips, slow strokes mixed with fast, quick ones, the taste of him warm on my
mouth, his body fitting against my own.

The hand that caressed my backside grew possessive again, and Dean
clenched me against him, pulling my hips against his hard cock and letting
me feel the length of it against the cradle of my sex. I whimpered into his
mouth at the sensation, and he only groaned harder, rolling me onto my
back and rolling atop me, his hips sliding against my own. His leg nudged
between mine, and I suddenly found myself with my legs spread wide
underneath him, his cock resting against my mound with scorching heat,
his mouth devouring my own. Excited by that, I rose my hips slightly,
bucking against him in a suggestive manner.

"Oh Jeezus, Abby. God help me when you do that," Dean said hoarsely
against my mouth, his hand sliding over my torso frantically.

In response, I swirled my hips against his again. "Don't tell me what
to do, Dean. You know I'll just prove you wrong," I teased, and nipped
against his bottom lip.

He groaned again, sliding down my body slightly to rest his head on my
sarong-covered stomach. He bit at the fabric, at my flat stomach underneath, and then slid down further, bunching the fabric up around my waist
as he went.

"Dean," I squeaked, shifting as his breath fanned hot on the most
intimate part of my body. "Are you sure you want to…" my voice trailed
off. I wasn't used to the oral sex for me before I went down on my partner.
Normally it was the other way around—I'd give out a dozen blowjobs long
before my date would ever think of reciprocating. Not to mention, other
than the shower last night, I'd been the most unkempt I'd ever been in my
life. The urge to cross my legs was strong—but that would have trapped
Dean's shoulders right where he wanted them.

In response to my worries, Dean licked the seam of my thigh, and a full-body, delicious shudder went through me. "You okay, Abby? Do you want me to stop?"

I sure didn't. My fingers twined in his messy hair and I let my legs slide open, bonelessly. "Hell no. Don't stop."

Dean chuckled, and the sound whispered across sensitive skin, and I sucked in a breath again. "You want me to keep going?" His thumb moved down my slit, and I bit my lip to keep from gasping. And when I gave him no response to his touch, he moved in. His mouth, hot and wet, found the sensitive bud of my clit, and I was lost. My entire body shuddered with every tongue flick, with every sucking motion, every rasp of his tongue.

Hips bucking in time with the swirl of his mouth, my legs began to tense with the onset of a powerful orgasm, and I panicked and began to pull away, self-conscious. In response to that, Dean locked his hands around me and pushed back, tonguing me so hard I swore I felt it down to my bones. With a gasping cry, I came in his arms, shudders wracking me as he continued to lap at me as if I were his breakfast, and he had all the time in the world.

"Oh my god," I breathed, unable to resist rotating my hips with his mouth one more time.

"Call me Dean," he teased, sliding up back over me and grinning as if he'd just been the one to fall to pieces, not me. His hand smoothed up and down over my hip, sliding into my sarong to tickle the tip of my breast. "Ready for round two, or do you need a breather?"

I gave him a puzzled look. "Why would I need a breather?"

The expression on Dean's face was downright innocent. "Shanna told me you weren't in great shape and I—"

My fists flew at him and I laughed, even as he grabbed me around the waist and pulled me toward him. I went easily, linking my arms around his neck and moving in for another deep kiss. I could taste myself on his mouth, a salty tang. "You are the sweetest thing, Abby. Like you were dipped in honey."

It was a terribly corny line. Sweet, but corny. I still fell for it. With a wicked grin, I gave him a push, indicating he should lay back on the bed. Dean did so, trying to pull me over him, but I wiggled away, pressing my palms on his chest to hold him down. "My turn." I slid down his body.

Dean froze under me, and I could see the wheels turning in his mind as he went over our conversation, trying to figure out if he'd suggested that

I reciprocate on him. "Abby," he began, then licked his lips, his breath coming out in a little pant. "I didn't mean…you don't have to…"

"I know," I said, sliding down until I straddled his calves. "Now shut up." I leaned forward, the tips of my breasts brushing against the hair on his legs. Dean groaned low in his throat, his hand sliding to my hair and twining there. Not pushing my head towards his cock, but a simple gesture of need. It was something I wanted to do, though—I wanted to drive him crazy as much as he'd driven me, and so I knelt over him, letting my hair fall against the thick length of his cock. His skin smelled musky so close to mine, and the scent of it sent a ripple through my body.

I grasped him in my hand, testing the heavy length. Hot and rigid, his cock was a sheath of silk over firm muscle, and I leaned over, fascinated, to dip my tongue against the head of it.

Dean groaned loudly, his hips jerking.

My, that was encouraging. I smiled at that—what fun. Slowly, languidly, as if I were licking an ice cream, I teased the head of his cock. Small, teasing licks. Deep, sensual licks. Playful, swirling licks. Drops of wetness appeared on the head, and I licked those off as well, then circled my thumb against the tip of his cock while I laved up and down the thick length.

His fist in my hair grew tighter as the minutes passed. "Jesus, Abby," he groaned at one point. "Have mercy."

"I have none," I teased, nipping lightly at the thick vein on the underside of his cock. Gently, with my lips and tongue alone. Then, with slow, languid motions, I circled the base of it with my fingers and slid my mouth over the rest of it, taking the length of him deep into my mouth.

"Christ," he exploded, grabbing me by the shoulders and pulling me off of him. I laughed until he tossed me underneath him, sliding my hips apart, and I thought he was going to plunge into me right then and there, and my breath caught in my throat. But he only pushed me down onto the bed and pressed a kiss to my mouth. "Wait here," he said against my lips, and I squirmed on the bed, waiting, as he disappeared into the bathroom and returned a moment later with a condom.

And then he was down over my body again, and kissing my face and neck as the condom crinkled between our bodies, and I watched him roll it down over his cock. He leaned in for one last kiss before nudging the head of his cock against my sex, then sinking deeply. I sucked in a deep breath even as he growled above me, hands grasping my hips sharply as he pulled back and then plunged again.

"Sexy little Abby in her pink bikini," he said in a low, growly voice even as thrust again. "Thank god you picked me again. It'd been a real shame—" A hard, rocking thrust—" if you never showed me that sweet little body of yours." Another rough thrust, one that made my breath catch in my throat.

I gave him a throaty laugh, my hips rising to meet each thrust, legs locked around his waist. "You're the one... that walked into my shower... remember?"

He grinned at that, and gave me another slow, rocking thrust and leaned forward, stretching my legs wide as he leaned in to kiss me. "I surely do," he drawled, taking my ankle and hooking it behind his neck, and thrusting again with that slow, sensuous motion that was going to twist me into one big orgasmic knot. Again he thrust, and again, and my body arched slightly higher with each silken stroke. And when one of his hands that had been gripping my hip slipped free and sought the damp curls of my sex, I moaned his name and dug my fingernails into his shoulder as I came, shuddering. After that, Dean seemed to lose all control, thrusting relentlessly into my body until he was racked by shudders as well, a hoarse shout on his lips as he came, collapsing over me.

I pressed a kiss to his scratchy face with its two-week growth of dark blonde beard. "Think we can stay here forever?"

He chuckled at that, propping up on his elbows so he didn't crush me under his weight and brushing a damp lock of hair off of my forehead. "We can't stay here. If we don't go back, we don't win the money."

Oh yes, the money. I made a face against the warm heat of his chest wall. The money that the producers would make sure that I would not get. The money that was Dean's driving urge to be here. For some reason, that made me a little sad—the others had seemed greedy and driven, but for some reason I'd held Dean to a different standard. I shrugged my shoulders against his damp body, listening to the racing of his heart as it slowed down. I hadn't given the money much thought in the past few days—my mind was consumed with the blonde god that I shared my beach with.

"Besides," he whispered against my forehead, pressing a kiss to my eyebrow. "If we don't get up now, we don't get to eat our breakfast."

I jumped at that, wriggling out from underneath him and straightening my sarong. It had fallen apart on me, and I re-wrapped it as I moved toward the door "Breakfast?"

Dean laughed behind me. "Thrown over for pancakes and bacon. Figures."

"Oh my god, they have bacon?" I squealed, running forward. "Bacon and showers. I'm the luckiest girl ever."

"And a hot guy in your bed," Dean prompted, moving to pick a sausage link off the table and closing his eyes with delight at the taste. "Okay, never mind—the food is better than sex."

I laughed, grabbing one of the pancakes—no syrup—and waving it at him. "You're just saying this because you want me to stuff a couple of pancakes down my bra."

His eyes lit up at the same time mine did.

AFTER ONE MORE QUICK SHOWER AND A HASTY RE-DRESSING, THE production crew knocked on our door. I moved slowly after Dean as they led us back to the helicopter, my bra stuffed with pancakes and a makeshift napkin-padded baggy of cold sausage and cheeses down the front of my bikini bottom. It was kind of disgusting if you sat and thought about it, but when you were starving, you did what you had to do—and that included sneaking food back to the island in your panties. Luckily, my sarong was heavily wrinkled and voluminous and hid everything.

I felt a keen sense of disappointment when the boat pulled up to shore and our camp came into view. I didn't want to go back—back to biting bugs and sand in everything and no showers and starving. But Dean squeezed my hand as we got off the boat, and I followed behind him because I wasn't quite ready to leave him just yet, either. No matter how much of a knee-jerk reaction I had to returning to the island.

A camera-man circled nearby as we trudged back to our beach, me with my arm crossed over my chest to keep my pancakes in place, my other hand still firmly latched into Dean's. To my surprise, two people sat at our camp on our chairs (well, logs that passed as chairs). "Are they filming?" I asked Dean, squinting my eyes. I couldn't see cameras with them. The sun was high in the sky, nearly blinding me, but I couldn't raise my arm to shield my eyes or risk losing my pancakes.

His steps slowed in front of me, to the point that I almost ran into his back. "It's Lana...and Leon, if I'm judging by the tattoos."

Lana and...Leon? I felt a surge of disappointment, though I kept it out of my voice. "Oh? What about Will?"

"I don't see him." Dean didn't sound thrilled either, but his voice remained even, and he raised a hand to wave at them, even as he spoke to me. "Did you hide the peanut butter before we left?"

"Yeah—I buried it. Just in case."

He glanced back at me and touched my cheek. "Good girl." He seemed as if he wanted to do more, but then Dean released my hand and put his hands on my shoulders, his gaze flicking to my sarong. "Still got the food?"

I nodded.

"Still trust me?" He searched my face, a little anxious. "Because you're not going to like my suggestion."

I gave him a faint smile. "This involves our pancakes, doesn't it?"

Dean winked at me, and my heart sank when he said, "If we share with Lana, it'll cement our alliance. I'll buy you pancakes every morning if one of us wins the millions."

Yeah, but only one of us could win and it wasn't going to be me. Still, I was full from dinner and the breakfast this morning, and Lana was starting to look downright bony. I wouldn't have been able to eat in front of her anyhow. So I just gave Dean's hand a squeeze and nodded.

We approached the others and Lana gave a happy squeal of delight at the sight of us, extending her arms out and crossing the beach to hug us. "Dean! Abby! Look at you both! You're so clean!"

Leon followed a few steps behind her, clearly not as comfortable, but willing to fake it. He held a hand out to Dean and they shook, clapping each other on the shoulder in a warm greeting. Lana hugged me and when Leon moved forward to do the same, I took a step backward and began to fish the pancakes out of my top.

"Abby brought food back for you," Dean explained, glancing over at me. "She smuggled it in."

Lana's hands flew to her head. "Oh my god." Her eyes went wide. "You're kidding me. Food?"

I pulled out the pancakes and handed two to her, the other two to Leon. It was a little bizarre, since the pancakes were still warm from being cradled against my skin. "This is the only way we could think to smuggle them out," I said, but my words fell on deaf ears. Both Lana and Leon had crammed their mouths full before I could even finish the sentence.

Of course, if I'd been in their position, I'd probably have done the same thing. What was a little body rubbing when you were starving?

I thought their eyes were going to roll out of their heads when I reached under my sarong and pulled out the second package—sausage links and cold bacon, quadruple-wrapped in fabric napkins from the table.

"Was that where I think it was?" Leon asked in-between bites of pancake.

"I wrapped it nice and tight, so it's not like it really touched me," I said, pulling the fabric layers away to demonstrate.

"If you guys don't want to eat it, I will. I certainly don't mind where it's been," Dean offered.

For some reason, that made my face flare bright red, and I averted my eyes as Lana's gaze widened on me, then flicked back to Dean, then back to me again.

The last of the food was divvied up, and Dean and I watched as Lana and Leon made short work of the remaining sausages and cheese. When the food was gone, Lana licked her fingertip and retrieved every crumb from the bag, and we laughed at the sight. Strangely enough, that small bit of food bonded us, and there were smiles on all of our faces by the time Lana licked her thumb and gave one final sigh.

"Why don't you guys go and grab some more water?" Lana suggested. "Abby and I will stoke up the fire."

Leon gave Lana a meaningful look and then turned and clapped Dean on the back. "Sounds good to me. You want to show me where your well is, just in case?"

"Just in case of what?" I retorted, but Lana linked her arm in mine and began to drag me back to camp. I cast a helpless look at Dean, but he winked at me and clapped Leon on the back, and they left camp. They headed down the beach together, their heads together in discussion. Dean's hands waved as if he were measuring something, and I guessed that the conversation was all about food. Figured.

Lana seemed rather quiet as she prodded the fire, but that wasn't so unusual. I slunk down on one of the logs that passed as benches and sighed. Already I missed the beach house.

She cast a sly glance over at me. "So how was it?"

I propped my chin up on my fists and grinned. "The reward? It was really nice."

"No, I meant sleeping with Dean. How was it?"

I sucked in a breath, not expecting that. Had we been so obvious? We weren't holding hands when we got off the boat, and it's not like we'd kissed each other. I thought we were being fairly normal in front of them. "I'm not sure what you mean," I began.

Lana snorted at my hedging. "You blush every time you look at him now. And he looks at you like you're his property. He didn't look at you that way before. Wasn't hard to guess."

"Nothing happened," I protested.

"Was there alcohol? I'd have guessed that the producers tried to set up a romantic interlude. Easy to do when you're drunk."

I clamped my jaws shut and refused to answer, staring hard at the sorry fire. Lana still couldn't make a fire quite like I could. I took one of the sticks and adjusted the heavy log on top to allow more air to get to the coals beneath.

"Oh, Abby," she said in a disappointed voice. "He's playing for two million dollars, girlfriend. Don't make more of this than it is. He's just using you because you're a vote for him."

"That's not what it was like," I said stiffly. A small, angry part of me was horrified that she'd even think that I was stupid enough to fall for something like that. Or better yet, that no one could possibly be interested in me for me, just for what I could do for him. She hadn't been there. "You don't know Dean like I do."

Her smile was wry and a bit sad as she came to sit next to me on the log. She nudged me with her elbow. "So tell me, then. Tell me what you know about him that's different from what I know."

My mouth went dry. "He doesn't have a girlfriend—"

"That he told you about," she interjected smoothly. "Guys will say anything to get laid."

I threw my hands up in the air. "Why am I bothering to explain anything to you? You're determined to think he's a sleazeball and I'm an idiot, right? So it doesn't matter what I say at this point."

She grabbed my hand and dragged it back down, then squeezed it to get my attention. "Hey, hey. I'm just trying to be the big sister looking out for you."

"That's ironic," I said in a sulky tone. "I probably weigh double what you do."

"And you're about a foot taller," she agreed.

A smile touched the edges of my mouth and I buried my head in my hands. "Oh god, I hope I didn't make a stupid mistake. I really, really like him."

"If he's half the guy you say he is, and you like him, go for it." Her tiny hand patted me on the back. "I could be wrong about this kind of thing. You never know."

I desperately hoped she was.

"Besides," she continued. "Look at it this way. As long as you're sucking his dick, you'll have his vote if he makes it to the jury before you do."

"Lana!"

"I'm kidding, I'm kidding." She chuckled and gave me a hug. "Man, who'd have thought that your team would be the one to hook up? I totally did not call that."

"Me either," I agreed, shaking my head. "It just kind of happened, you know?"

"That's usually how they go," she agreed, digging her toes in the sand next to my own. "I'm not going to say anything to Leon, though."

Relief shot through me. "Thanks."

"Nothing to it. I've pulled him into our little alliance, but as far as he knows, Will isn't part of it. It's just you me and Dean. Now we're four strong, but Will is with us. And when we get to the merge, we'll have control." Her eyes gleamed in a predatory way. "And we can pick them all off and waltz right to the millions."

Chapter Ten

*When we first got stranded, I kept thinking about my next meal.
Now all I keep thinking about is when I get to touch Abby again.
I'm starting to hate when the others come over to our campsite.*
—*Dean Woodall, Day 18*

SOMETHING ABOUT LANA'S CALCULATED CHESS MOVES THROUGH THE game bothered me, but I kept quiet. When she drew Dean aside and told him her plan and he was equally enthusiastic, I kept my fears to myself. Maybe I was just being a chicken—but something about pulling in so many people bothered me. Perhaps because I was afraid that the more people in our alliance, the less valuable each member was. Still, you had to make big moves to get to the end, and Lana was definitely making some smart moves. I had to admire her for that.

Dusk fell and eventually Lana and Leon moved back to their own campsite, waving at us until the darkness swallowed them up.

No sooner did they leave than Dean grabbed me and pulled my body against his, his mouth hot on my own. "Thank Christ. I thought they'd never leave." His hands slid to my ass, cupping it and pulling me against him.

Well, at least Dean and I were on the same page. My worries momentarily put aside, I wrapped my arms around his neck and drew him down to me, licking the edges of his mouth. He tasted slightly salty this time, tangy with the sea around us, and bits of sandy grit rubbed between our bodies as we pressed against each other.

And then I winced as I watched a fat mosquito land on my arm. I jerked away from him, slapping at the creature. "God, I wish we were back in our cabin."

"Are you kidding? This gives me the perfect chance to oil you up," Dean said with a grin. He took my hand in his and led me around the campfire into the bushes, where he'd hidden our prized bug repellent. As he leaned over, I caught a perfect view of his lean, tight ass and slapped it.

Dean jerked back up, surprised.

"Mosquito," I said innocently.

"I'll bet," he said in a low, husky voice. He held up the jar and shook it. "Guess this means you'll be doing me first, doesn't it?"

Now that was an appealing offer. I took the jar and poured a little of the thick, creamy oil into my hand and set it back down on one of our makeshift benches. With a teasing look at Dean, I twirled my finger. "Turn around, sir."

He did, and my mouth nearly went dry at the sight of his broad shoulders. We were both starving down to nothing so his shoulder-blades were a little more prominent, but his waist was lean and taut, and the heavy triangle of his shoulders as healthy and gorgeous as ever. I wanted to run my tongue over his skin instead of the lotion, but I forced myself to behave. To warm the lotion, I rubbed both my hands together, and then placed them against his back, sliding over the play of muscles.

Dean gave a groan of pleasure. "This going to turn into an impromptu shoulder rub?"

"If you're lucky," I teased back.

"I feel pretty lucky right now," he said, and his light chuckle made my knees turn to jelly. I finished smoothing lotion down his spine and slid my hands up to his shoulders, my slick fingers gliding over the skin lightly. I kneaded his muscles for a few moments, then couldn't resist trailing my fingers down his corded arms. Muscular and tight, but not bulging. Just the way I liked it. I made a small noise of approval low in my throat and continued to slide my fingers down his arm, circling his wrist and then toying with his fingers.

"My front is getting lonely," he said in a hoarse voice, as affected by my light teasing as I was.

"Give it a minute," I said, leaning over his arm to whisper in his ear. "The mosquitos will all congregate there now that your back is safe."

He turned and grabbed my hand, then pulled me toward him. "Cruel woman." His mouth nipped at mine in a teasing fashion. "Just means I'll have to wear something over my front to cover it. I'm thinking a hot brunette with long legs and a smart mouth."

"I happen to know just the one," I responded, then bit his lower lip gently. My hands slid over his slick arms, trying to find purchase and just sliding over glossy, hard muscle. It only turned me on more. I took a step back from him and splayed my oily hands over his chest, pretending to glide more of the oil on his body, when all I really wanted to do was keep touching him. My palms slid over his collarbone as he stood stock still, moving down the line of his belly and gliding over his nipples.

He groaned at that and his hands tangled in my hair, pulling me in for a fast, passionate kiss. "Your turn. Give me your back."

I turned obediently—eagerly—and my stomach began to do a wild flip-flop of anticipation. I heard Dean opening the jar and pulled my thick, curly hair up in one hand so it wouldn't get into the oil when he put it on my back. And then I waited.

And waited.

Seconds ticked by like hours, and I squirmed in place, turned on and anxious all at once. He wasn't having second thoughts, was he—

Warm, slick hands slid over my shoulders, and I nearly melted onto the sand.

It felt amazing. The few back massages I'd had before had never been particularly relaxing—most guys tended to dig in their fingers in a way that was painful instead of pleasant, but Dean knew just how to touch me. His fingers glided over my skin, brushing against the straps of my bikini and fluttering underneath. He pressed down ever so slightly, kneading the muscles as he stroked, and worked over my shoulders and the top of my spine, and then slid further down to the small of my back and stroked over the skin on my hips and belly, his arms snaking around like a caress as he touched me. I shivered when he hit a ticklish spot, but I didn't ask him to stop.

His oily hands brushed against the elastic of my bikini bottom, hinting at things to come, and I turned in his arms, my breath fluttering in my throat. "Got to do my front first," I whispered.

Dean pulled me back against him and my body slid against his slick one. "Let's go to the shelter," he said. "Private there." And he gave me a kiss to appease my sudden frown.

I wasn't frowning at the thought of having to wait the short distance (like thirty feet) to get to the shelter—I was frowning at the thought of the camera crews possibly watching us grease each other up and how turned on we were getting. It was a private moment on an island where there weren't any, and I peered suspiciously at the shadows. "Did you see a camera man?" They were so unobtrusive and quiet that I'd stopped noticing them after the first few days. I kicked myself mentally—how could I forget where we were?

"No, but I want to be sure that there's no surprise cameras hidden in the trees," Dean said, and relief spiraled through me. He linked his hand in mine and grabbed the jar with his other, leading me back to the shelter. "Guess what I stole from our cabin," Dean said to me with a grin.

I couldn't guess. "What?"

He pressed the jar against his pocket, and I heard foil crinkle. Condoms. Clever man.

I grinned at that and moved to the front of our shelter. "Glad we didn't share those with the other team." We kept a few extra palm fronds near the front of the shelter to wipe the sand off of our feet, and as we did so, I noticed something odd. "Our shelter—they expanded it while we were gone."

Dean grunted at that. "Yeah, Lana was mentioning something about it. Said it was too cramped for two adults."

For some reason, that made me sad. "I kind of liked cramped." Now I didn't have an excuse to snuggle up against Dean through the night, and I actually wanted to.

"Me too," Dean said, and his voice sounded just as put out as my own, which made me grin. Then he slapped me on the behind. "Ladies first. Get in there so I can finish you off."

The double entendre wasn't lost on me. I made sure to wiggle my ass as I crept into the small shelter.

Lana had definitely been busy. The interior of our tiny shelter had been expanded—where before we'd barely managed to squeeze two bodies on four bamboo planks, we had ten now. She'd taken my original A-frame shelter and expanded it with a second A-frame, and had a heavy bough of leaves crisscrossing the middle. It was a lot like an M without the dip in the middle.

"I need to thank her tomorrow," I said, pulling my legs under me and reaching for our one lonely blanket that was folded in the corner.

"There's one thing I like about this," Dean said, crawling in behind me, and he pulled something over the front, blocking out the view of the sky. "She actually made a door, that crazy woman."

I glanced at the other side of the frame behind me and sure enough, she'd created a flap to cover the entrance. "Definitely have to thank her tomorrow."

Dean grabbed my ankle and tucked it over his shoulder, and I fell back onto my elbows. In the low light, I could just barely catch a glimpse of his devilish smile. "Lay back, my lady, and let your humble manservant oil up thine legs."

"Humble manservant? Where has he been all this time?"

"Busy admiring the view," Dean said in the worst cockney accent I'd ever heard.

I was about to tease him about it when instead of oiling up my leg, he twisted his body around so that he was on his knees, my foot still over his shoulder, and he knelt between my legs. He grabbed my other calf and pulled it up until I was spread out on the floor, Dean looming over me and biting at my lower belly with his teeth.

"Dean!" I gasped as he began to tug my bikini bottom down with his fingers, momentarily jerking my legs together. He left it dangling on one foot over his shoulder and moved in, nuzzling at my thigh. I squirmed, trying to keep my moans muffled as he moved ever closer towards the spot I needed him at the most. "We shouldn't," I began to protest, and then moaned loudly when his breath fanned across my slit, my hips bucking slightly.

"Hush, woman. I'm busy renewing my alliance with my team-mate. I need to win her over if I want her to vote for me," he said in a husky voice, and his tongue slid lightly along the seam of my skin, already damp. His fingers slid my folds apart, and then his mouth moved over my flesh, and I lost the tart reply I'd come up with as his tongue grazed my clit.

And after a few seconds, I didn't care if the cameras in the forest caught my cries of pleasure after all.

I STARED DOWN THE ENDLESS, SANDY BEACH AND HAD TO FORCE MYSELF not to touch Dean. The others lined up on the sand next to us, and as usual, curious glances were being directed our way. I knew they were waiting to see if we'd explode on each other, but the ruse was getting harder and harder to keep up, and I felt their scrutiny intensely.

Next to me, tall and tense, Dean had his arms crossed over his chest, watching our host with intensity. If he felt the same awkwardness that I did, he hid it amazingly well.

Down the row, Lana seemed to sense my awkwardness, and she gave me a long, meaningful look and a slight tip of her chin, as if saying *straighten out. Head in the game.*

I nodded at her and turned my focus back to Chip. Focus.

"This is your final team challenge," Chip said in a boisterous voice, as if he were more excited about that than we were. He held up a colorful length of rope. "This will tie you to your team-mate, and together, tied at the waist, you will both make your way through the most grueling obstacle course imaginable."

Oh gee. Great.

"This last challenge is, of course, for immunity. The two teams that finish last will be taken to Judgment, where one team will be eliminated."

The last one. We just had to get through this one, and we'd made it past the first round. After that, it would be individual challenges, and our secret alliance would quietly clean up behind the scenes. I wanted to look over at Dean and see if he was relieved or unhappy that we'd soon be lumped in with everyone else, but I didn't dare glance over.

I remained calm and silent as I was lashed to Dean's side with a bright red bungee cord of some kind. It separated us by about a foot—just enough so that we'd trip over each other—and had a bit of give, but not enough. I could quickly see how the producers wanted this challenge to go—one partner dragging the other through the obstacle course. Lovely. I peeked ahead at the obstacles through the trees—yup, sure enough, I could see some sort of swinging vine and a pool of mud up ahead.

Poor Dean, stuck with me.

"Teams ready?" Chip shouted, dragging my attention back, and as a one we hunched forward, one knee placed in front of the other, readying to run.

"Last two teams across the finish head to Judgment," Chip lowered his arm. "Good luck! Go go go!"

The teams surged into action. Dean and I surged forward as well. The rope tying my waist to Dean's jerked as he leapt ahead, and I had to scramble to keep my feet, the breath sucking out of my lungs. Adrenaline rushed through me and I began to charge forward. I wanted to beat the others at their game, suddenly—show them that Dean and I truly were a force to be reckoned with.

And I really, really did not want to go home tonight.

The first obstacle was a low climbing wall, and the teams crammed together, pushing and jostling to try and get over—not an easy feat considering we were lashed together. Dean was right at my back and nudging my shoulder, and as soon as I felt an ounce of give in the rope, I began to climb, swinging my legs over.

I still wasn't much of an athlete, but the rush coursing through me helped. I managed to wobble my way down the other side without more than a skinned knee as I fell forward. Dean grabbed me by the arm and helped me back to my feet and we charged forward.

It wasn't long before we were ahead of the other teams by a long shot. No surprise, really—Dean was so athletic he was dragging me along when I faltered, and his momentum spurred me on. We'd also had protein (the peanut butter) to fuel us. I was hanging in with him, while my other female competitors seemed to be wilting. Even Lana, who was quick and fast thanks to her tiny frame, wasn't quite keeping up with Leon.

We were going to win again. Joy surged through me, and I grabbed onto the rope, trying to urge Dean forward. The line of obstacles continued—a rope net, another wall climb, and a digging challenge. Dean seemed full of endless energy, and as other people caught up with us and then fell behind again, pride surged through me. I watched his shoulders flex, tawny with the sun and gleaming with sweat.

Perhaps I was a little too focused on watching my partner, because after we both grabbed onto a knotted rope swing and flung ourselves over a mud pit. I landed on my ankle.

There was a nasty pop as my weight landed awkwardly on my foot and pain shot through my leg. I yelped and collapsed, and the short length of rope ensured that Dean fell on me. Pain—red and blinding—flared, and I nearly blacked out.

Dean cursed as he pushed off of me, not realizing how hurt I was. "Get up, Abby. We almost have this!"

The pain was blinding, but some stupid part of me was rushing with adrenaline, and at his urging hands, I tried to stand on my foot anyhow... and promptly fell to the ground again as white-hot pain shot through me. Dean fell back over me again.

As we fell back to the ground, I saw the first team rush past us, heading for the finish. It was close.

"My ankle," I said, my voice sounding too close to tears. "I can't walk."

"We have to finish or we'll be eliminated," Dean said, trying to help me up. "You have to try and walk. Just a few feet."

I nodded and leaned on Dean, trying to shift my weight so I could limp along with him. We did that for a few moments. One team whizzed past us, then another. I made a frustrated sound in my throat, and Dean sucked in a breath. He was thinking the same thing I was—if we were one of the last two teams, we'd be on the chopping block. The last place I wanted us to be. But I couldn't seem to swallow the agony. The white hot pain was overriding all rational thought, and I leaned heavily on him.

Another moment later, Dean hesitated. I thought he was going to get mad at me for my slow limping, but to my surprise, he swung me up in his arms. "It's okay, baby," he whispered and pressed his mouth to my hair, hauling me into his arms. "Almost done." And I buried my face in his chest as he carried me across the finish line, limping heavily into last place.

All my fault.

I HUNG MY HEAD AT THE COUNCIL OF JUDGMENT AS CHIP STOOD IN THE front, ready to read the votes. The questions we'd received from him hadn't been warm, and had mostly been about how I was dragging my team down. There wasn't a lot of sympathy in the faces of my other competitors, either. One or two had a look of glee on their faces, though they'd tried to hide it. After all, I was pretty much out of the water in any sort of physical challenge. The last team immunity and I'd lost it for Dean.

I *sucked.*

My ankle was wrapped tightly but swollen to twice the size. As soon as the cameras had stopped rolling for the competition, medical had swooped in and checked me out. The verdict? A bad sprain but no breaks, so I was left in the game, unless I chose to bail out (and thereby drag Dean into the loser lodge involuntarily). I chose to stay.

Even if it was just until Judgment.

Jack and Meg sat next to us on the Elimination Bench, and they seemed quite a bit more confident than Dean and myself. After all, they were both whole. They'd had trouble working together to cross the mud pond with the rope swing and had ended up wading through. Their clothes were still dark and covered with mud, but they seemed confident as they flicked glances over at me and my monstrous ankle.

"Teams, pass your slates forward. I'll read the first vote," Chip said in his best TV-host voice. He pulled up the first slate, regarded it, and then flipped it as he read the name.

"Team Six."

I regarded the slate with mixed emotions. The next would be for us, for sure. Dean was a strong competitor.

Chip held up the second slate. "Team Six."

I sat up a little at that, surprised. I glanced over at Lana, who sat in the audience, and she gave me a meaningful look, her eyes hard. Had she orchestrated something quietly at Judgment council to save our asses? I would so have to thank her when we got back if that was the case. She could eat all my peanut butter if she wanted it.

Well, maybe not that.

She was stone-faced as they read the next vote. "Team Six" but I noticed the faint hint of a smug smile on her partner Leon's face. Further down the row, Will was openly smiling, his arms crossed over his chest.

Sure enough, Lana had saved our asses. I owed her.

Dean seemed to realize the same thing, slowly. He sat up straighter as the last two votes were read, and I glanced over at him and smiled, delighted, and reached for his hand. I wanted to hug him, but such a brash display of affection would work against us.

Apparently Dean felt that any sort of affection would work against us. He pulled his hand out of mine and gave me a hard frown.

I pulled back away, trying to brush it off, but his cold rebuff had hurt my silly, stupid feelings. I bit the inside of my cheek to keep from crying. It was stupid but my ankle hurt, my pride was wounded, and my emotions were completely strung out. I wanted Dean to hold me, not rebuff me. I glanced over at Lana to see if she'd seen my small gesture as well.

She had. The look on her face had turned hard and unfriendly. She didn't approve of my needy actions.

"Team Eleven! You live for another round," Chip crowed as he moved over to us and helped me to my feet. "How do you feel?"

"Ready to keep playing," Dean said in his smooth, effortlessly cocky voice.

"Great," I added, forcing a smile to my face.

WITH THE HELP OF A SHIRT-WRAPPED STICK ACTING AS MY CRUTCH, WE were able to hobble back into camp once the boat dropped us off. Dean hadn't said much to me, which was just as well—I wasn't in the mood to talk to him either. All of my energy was going into walking without maiming myself further.

When we made it back to camp, I sat heavily on a log and put my head in my hands, frustrated. Frustrated at myself for screwing up in the challenge, frustrated that I'd tried to be needy with Dean and he'd turned me away because it was the smart thing to do. Frustrated because Lana had noticed and she was unhappy with me. This day had been one big mess of crap from the start.

To my surprise, Dean sat next to me and began to brush the hair off my shoulders, rubbing the frustrated knot at the base of my neck. "How are you holding up?"

"I feel stupid," I admitted. "I almost blew it for us." I decided not to bring up the part about him rebuffing me in front of the others. It was stupid to get hurt feelings over it.

"It happens." He pulled me into his lap, careful of my injured foot, and began to nibble on my neck. "Don't beat yourself up."

"Too late," I said in a grumpy voice, but twined my arms around his neck and leaned in so his lips could have better access to my skin.

His lips moved to mine and his tongue slid along the crease of my mouth. I parted to let him in and his tongue flicked against mine, and a small moan rose in my throat, making me forget about my wounded ankle. He groaned low and slid his hands to my hips, shifting me in his arms. His hips lifted against my own in a suggestive move. "Can you slide your leg over?" he breathed against my mouth, and then bit at my lower lip, as if his mouth couldn't stand to be parted from mine for a single moment.

Sounded like a good idea to me. With his hands on my hips to steady me, and my hands on his shoulders, we maneuvered a little awkwardly, watching for my injured foot. After a bit of awkward maneuvering, I was able to straddle him as he sat on the log, and the cradle of my sex was firmly slid up against the hard length of his. It felt enormous and hot even through his swim trunks, and I flexed my hips forward and was delighted to hear his breath suck in. he grasped my ass and ground me down against his cock and his mouth lowered to nuzzle my breast through my bikini. I gasped as his mouth grazed my nipple and twined my fingers in his hair to hold him in place, my eyes focused on his intense, handsome face. His short buzz of dark ash blonde hair was growing out and it stuck up from his head like a spiky bed of grass.

Something moved behind his head. I glanced up, just as he pushed aside the fabric of my bikini, exposing my nipple and placed his mouth on it again.

The moan of pleasure died in my throat at the sight of Lana and Leon heading down the beach toward us.

I grabbed at my bikini, nearly snapping his head backward.

"Abby, what—"

I wiggled on his lap, trying to extricate myself from his grasp before they could see us in such an obvious position and guess what we were up to.

Unfortunately, my hurt foot was seriously compromising my ability to move. I twisted on Dean helplessly for a few moments before he glanced over his shoulder and saw the same thing. "Shit." He stood up quickly, me still in his arms, and then set me down on the fallen log that served as our bench.

"I'm going to grab water," he said, leaving me alone on the log and swinging by the other side of the firepit to grab our water bucket. I was about to protest when I caught a glimpse of him in profile—and the massive tent he was sporting in the front of his swim trunks. All right, water was probably a smart move. Still, it left me stranded and breathless as I raised a hand to my eyes, squinting at the sunny beach as Lana and Leon approached.

Lana wore a scowl on her face as I greeted her, as if she'd guessed what we'd been up to and was mad at catching us red-handed again, like we were a couple of horny teenagers. Leon was far more blasé about it, to the point that I wondered if he'd seen anything. Both of them carried bags on their shoulders.

"Where's Dean?" Lana said in a sharp voice.

I cocked my head towards the dense jungle a few short steps away from the sandy encampment. "He went to get water. What's up?"

She glanced down at the front of my swimsuit and rolled her eyes. I quickly glanced down as well—on top of nipples that were standing at attention, I had a gigantic wet spot over one from Dean's mouth, directly in the center of the Y for 'ABBY'.

How embarrassing. Shoot me now, God. I colored and wished I could get up from my seat to grab my shirt. So instead, I crossed my arms over my chest and rubbed them as if pretending to be cold…in the hundred degree oppressive tropical heat. Yeah.

Leon looked at me like I was crazy. "You guys read your Tribal Summons yet?"

"Tribal Summons?" I glanced over at the treasure chest and sure enough, a long scroll was sticking out of one side, the lid ajar. Of course. The game went on, even if Dean and I were no longer paying attention. "My ankle injury kind of distracted us," I said, and stretched it out in front of me to remind them.

That changed the focus of the conversation entirely. Lana immediately sat down next to me and glanced at my ankle with a worried look. "How bad is it?"

"Sprain," I admitted. "I thought I'd broke it but the game doctors told me that if I keep my weight off of it, I should be able to walk within a week or so."

"A week!" Lana exclaimed, as if it was the end of the world.

"You gonna evac?" Leon asked me, standing over me and blotting out the sun with his huge tattooed shoulders. "Quit the game?"

"Me? No. I want to keep playing." The thought of quitting the game and screwing Dean over? Never crossed my mind. He wanted this badly and I wanted to spend time with him. Despite the bugs and the sand and the stress of the game, I was enjoying myself, oddly enough. "I'm in this to win it." Well, kind of. More like I was in this to pad my book deal.

Oddly enough, I hadn't thought about my book deal much since getting on the island and meeting Dean. Thinking about it now kind of made me feel…unclean. Like I was deceiving him. I didn't care for that much. Would he hold it against me once we were out of here?

Was there anything for us when we were out of here, I wondered. Why was I even thinking that?

Lana and Leon were still discussing my ankle, though. Did it hurt to walk? Did I think I'd be able to perform in challenges? What about helping out around camp? I endured their grilling, answering mostly with "I don't know" and "Yes, but it hurts". Lana finally revealed the reason behind her grilling. "Leon's joined our alliance," she revealed. I glanced up at the big tattooed guy and he nodded at me.

"I'll have to tell Dean," I murmured, not sure what to think of this. Another person? We had five for sure, then, if Will was still with us. "Do you think the other five have allied?"

"Nope," said Leon. "Shanna's on my team and we haven't been approached by anyone. She'll vote with me when the next Judgment comes."

So that was six, really. That sure seemed like a lot of people if only ten were left. I said nothing though, since Lana was running the show and she seemed utterly confident in her actions. "So what's the plan?"

"We're merging, which you would know if you had checked your Island Mail," she said with a pointed look at me that made me blush and cover my arms over my chest again. "That means ten of us, all on the same beach. With six of us voting together, that means we can pick off the other four."

It seemed like an obvious question, but I had to ask. "And what happens when we get down to six?"

"The big prizes come at the final four," she said, just as Dean reappeared from the underbrush, sweaty and carrying a bucket of water (and sans boner, thank goodness). "It'll be you, me, Leon and Dean to the four. We can decide who goes after that."

"What about Shanna and Will?"

"We don't tell them," Lana said with intense eyes as Dean moved toward us. "The final four pact stays with us here on this beach, since we won't have any privacy at the new camp."

"New camp?" Dean said, wiping at his forehead with his forearm. He flicked a concerned look over me, as if checking to see that I was doing okay, and then turned his focus back to Leon and Lana.

"We're merging," Leon said, gesturing at the Tribal Summons. Dean cast me a wary look and then pulled the chest open. Two bags—just like Lana and Leon's—were left for us, along with the long parchment scroll that told us of the merge and drew a map of the new campsite.

"It's a few miles down the beach," Dean said, and squinted at the blue line of water just off in the distance.

My heart sank at that. "A few miles?"

"I can carry you on my back," Leon said to me. "Won't be nothing."

"I'll be the one to carry Abby," Dean said, his voice taking on a sharp edge.

"It's not a big deal, man—"

"I'll do it," Dean said, and I could hear his teeth gritting. I imagined the mental image of me splayed across Leon's back, my breasts pressing up against his shoulders, legs wrapped around his hips. Dean apparently had the same mental image I did, and he didn't like it.

Dean moved to my side, as if to cement his claim. "If you guys can carry our bags…"

"Chill man," Leon said. "I already got a girl."

I blushed.

Lana looked like she wanted to murder all of us. "Can you guys stop thinking with your dicks for five minutes? We are here to win the money, not play Beach Blanket Bingo."

"Like I said," Dean drawled, helping me to my feet. "You guys carry our bags and we'll be just fine. We'll even bribe you," he said with a wink at me.

"The peanut butter?" I said slowly. I realized what he was doing—cementing our alliance at the last moment and bribing them to forget about the small spat that had just happened. Not to mention that we'd have to share the peanut butter with the others once we got to the beach anyhow. Best to fuel our alliance.

"You guys have peanut butter?" Lana whispered. Leon slapped Dean on the back, grinning his pleasure.

I nodded and pointed at where it was buried in the sand, a stick poking up to mark the spot. "We've been eating before challenges to stay strong. It was my reward item," I confessed.

"You lucky!" Lana exclaimed, her eyes wide.

Between the four of us, we quickly devoured the remaining peanut butter left in the jar. We'd carefully saved a third of it, and at Dean's meaningful glance, I hung back on the food and let Lana and Leon eat the lion's share, though it was hard to do so. My stomach grumbled at the rich peanut smell and I wanted to devour the whole thing on my own. Still, this was a game about allies, and mine were currently rather pleased with us.

"What about the bug oil?" Lana asked.

"Bringing that," Dean said, and moved to the shelter to pack our bags.

Our small bits of clothing were packed into one satchel, the other full of necessities from the camp—the cooking pot, the blanket, the plates we'd made out of shells. Once the stuff was bagged up, Leon belted Dean's machete at his waist and Dean hauled me onto his back. My legs stuck out from around his torso and I clung to his shoulders like he was giving me a piggyback ride. His feet shifted as he moved into the sand, and I was struck with a pang of guilt. "Going to be a long walk for you," I whispered in his ear as we began to head down the beach. Lana and Leon were a few paces ahead, double-bags on their shoulders as they studied the map.

"You're mine," Dean said simply. "I'm not about to hand you off to someone else."

I wondered at his choice of words.

Chapter Eleven

I'm thrilled that we merged. Thrilled. Can't you tell from the sound of my voice? No? Me either. I preferred when it was just us on the beach. Lots of alone time. —Dean Woodall, Day 20

WE STOPPED A FEW TIMES SO DEAN COULD REST, BUT HE INSISTED on being the one to carry me. It was just as well—Leon was sweating in the hot afternoon sun and I wasn't relishing the thought of rubbing up against him. Dean was sweating too, but leaning against his body and letting him carry me just let my wicked imagination run away with itself, to the point that I was ready to drag him behind the nearest tree and have my way with him.

If it weren't for the way that Lana kept looking back at us with a frown.

And the fact that we were meeting up with six other people who were about to share living space with us.

"Are you nervous about meeting the others?" I asked Dean as we approached the new camp. I could see people standing in the distance, and smelled the smoke of a fire. The sun was setting, so I couldn't make out who it was, though I knew the faces remaining in the game by now: Chris and Alys from Team 5 (both extremely athletic), Heather from Team 8 (the young, cute grad student), Riley whose profession I couldn't recall, but I remembered his freckled shoulders from other challenges, and of course Will and Shanna the Bunny. I was a little surprised she'd made it this far, but then again, she was probably good at latching on to a strong man— like Leon before the switch. She seemed to be good friends with Riley now, though she squealed with delight at the sight of Leon and rushed over to hug him as we arrived in camp. She also looked like nothing but skin and bones...and a large set of implants. The others just looked skinny in comparison.

They watched me with interest as Dean moved close to the fire and set me down gently, and then the introductions began. The men slapped Dean on the back and congratulated him on arriving, and the women hugged him. I kind of sat on the bench and watched, elevating my foot and trying not to look as awkward as I felt.

"Oh wow, you didn't evac?" Shanna said as she looked over at me. "I thought you broke your foot."

"Just a sprain," I repeated for the billionth time. "Should be better in a few days."

"Huh."

I couldn't tell if that was an insulting noise or an 'I underestimated you' noise. A few of the others crowded around as if just now noticing that I was here, but I noticed that Dean seemed to be the star of the show. I fielded questions about my ankle as I watched him, laughing and rubbing his shoulders where I'd leaned earlier for several hours. A camera-man hovered nearby, just on the fringes of camp, and I noticed the others paid no more attention to him than I did.

"We have a Tribal Summons," Heather said, waving the others to the back of the camp.

"Already?" said Chris.

"It looks like food!"

That was all it took for all of the remaining players to flood over to the edge of camp and head to the decorated, ornate trunk. In the darkness I couldn't see anything, and I couldn't get up to follow. Depressed, I noticed that not even Dean had hung around camp to see if I wanted to join them.

It was just a momentary slip, I reasoned, but it still stung. I stared at the flickering fire and ignored the camera-man as he zoomed in on my face. Stupid ankle. Stupid team not even noticing that I was here alone.

"Sandwiches! And champagne!" I heard Shanna squeal, and the others erupted into a flurry of conversation.

My stomach growled. I wanted to weep as I imagined them scarfing down the food, hands grabbing. Maybe someone would save me a sandwich.

A female giggle arose from the group. "Don't drink all of it now—save some for later!"

Sigh. Maybe not.

I supposed that I could call out and remind them that I was stuck here on the bench, but I kept my mouth shut. Arriving at camp had been a bit awkward—my foot injury had made them unsure of what to do with me. I had no doubt that if we were still playing on teams, I'd be voted off first. Now that we were all one big team and all challenges and rewards, I was pretty much safe—I'd be extremely safe, actually. I wasn't going to win any challenges on my own now, after all.

Safe as could be, as long as I didn't starve to death.

"Here," a familiar voice said, and I felt something cold touch my shoulder.

I jerked around in surprise and stared at the champagne bottle pressed against my skin, and Dean's grinning face.

"Thought I'd bring you something. There's enough for everyone, but not for long." In his other hand, he held out a large end of a massive sub sandwich.

Happiness swept over me as he sat next to me and handed me the sandwich. More than the food, it was that he hadn't forgotten me.

"Did I ever mention that you are my favorite man on the island?" I said as he offered the champagne to me and I took a swig. It tingled in my mouth, all fizz and alcohol, and it was lovely.

"I'd better be," is all he said, and we didn't talk as we ate the sandwich and drank more alcohol. I blushed at the meaningful look he gave me, wondering if he was feeling that same swelling in his heart that I was.

That swelling that told me that I was completely, ridiculously head over heels for the guy.

Eventually others trickled back to camp, eating their sandwiches and passing around more champagne. Bottle after icy bottle was produced from a cooler shaped to look like a treasure chest, and another two camera-men had arrived. I guessed what was going on—good TV was a bunch of starving idiots getting drunk on champagne and partying, and the team was all too willing to comply. Heck, I was too.

The revelry went on for a few hours, it seemed, until someone laughingly pointed out, "Hey, we have a new shelter."

All heads turned in that direction.

I was struck by a sudden bout of nervousness—who would be sleeping where? Luckily at that moment, no one seemed to be in much of a mood to sleep. They crawled all over the shelter, exploring and exclaiming over the fact that we had pillows—the first ones in three weeks. Instead, the drunks staggered over it and laughed, and then the partying continued.

My own head was feeling swimmy at the moment, the result of too much alcohol on too-starved and tired a body. I was feeling good, too, and I looked over at Dean and wished at that moment that we were alone together instead of stuck with all of these people.

He glanced over at me and seemed to share the same thought. Desire flicked across his face, then quickly concealed itself again. He glanced at the group, laughing and hanging all over each other. They were singing songs by the campfire, though a few less-hardy had collapsed in the shelter in the distance and were making use of the new pillows.

"Come on," he said in a low voice, and began to help me up from my seat. He gave me a meaningful look that made my body flare with need.

I leaned heavily on him and glanced at the others, wondering how we'd ditch them. Dean solved the problem, however. "I'm taking Abby to bed," he said to the group, who waved us off without looking back. And with that, he swept me into his arms and whispered, "They're too drunk to realize where we're really going, and by the time they do, it won't matter."

"Sounds good to me," I whispered back, trying to hide the nervous giggle that threatened to erupt. Sneaking away to have sex? It felt so very high school. And damn if I wasn't excited about it, too.

We barely made it into the bushes before Dean's mouth was hot on mine, tasting of champagne, the scent of Dean's skin—smoky and masculine— surrounded me.

"Look out for my ankle," I murmured against his mouth as he set me down on a nearby fallen coconut tree.

"I have no intention of forgetting any part of you," Dean said, kneeling between my spread knees. He crouched on the sand and stared up at me from between my thighs, a devilish grin on his face.

I clung to the tree for support when he began to tug off my bikini bottom. "What are you doing?"

His mouth pressed hot against my flesh as he bared it, his hands anchoring at my hips. "Team building exercise," he breathed against my belly.

"We're merged now," I protested weakly, scanning the tree-line in case one of our tribe mates went looking for us.

"Give me a minute," Dean said with a low chuckle. "We'll do all the merging you want."

I began to get caught up in the moment, especially when his mouth pressed a few more kisses on my inner thigh. My fingers tangled in his short hair, wild from our days on the island. "So what is this 'alliance' going to do for me, I wonder?"

"Let me show you," he said, and his mouth dipped lower.

"Wake up." Someone nudged my arm.

I mumbled, ducking my head under my arm to avoid the sunlight. The bed was so comfortable that I didn't want to get up. My head rested on a soft pillow and two warm bodies were pressed against both sides of me. Behind me, someone had their arm wrapped around my waist, and I heard the soft chatter of voices in the distance.

"Not just yet," I mumbled and snuggled deeper. "Five more minutes."

A hot mouth pressed to my bare shoulder. "Wakey wakey," Dean brushed his mouth against my skin.

My eyes flew open and I stared at the broad back that I was currently snuggled up against. Tattoos covered one arm and "LIVE FREE" was scrawled across the shoulder blades six inches from my nose.

Leon. With Dean behind me.

A bit unnerved at realizing that Leon had crawled next to me in my sleep (and that I'd cuddled up against his warmth), I sat up, pushing my curly hair out of my face and trying not to frown. Dean's hand lay low on my hip, resting possessively on me.

We were the only three left in the bed. I squinted at the distance, where the others stood near the fire, the early morning sunlight trickling in and bathing everyone in a dull gray pallor. Storm clouds had rolled in overnight, and the warm sun was hidden, leaving only storm clouds behind. One or two of the tribes mates in the distance didn't seem to be super chipper—Shanna held her head in her hands, probably the result of over-indulging last night.

I glanced over at Dean. He lay in the bed looking up at me with an amused face, his other arm tucked under his head. Beneath him, a thick bed of palm leaves had been crushed and trampled—probably by the rest of the tribe. He looked so sleepy and sexy that I wanted to run away from everyone else and do a repeat performance of last night's lovemaking.

"How's your ankle?"

I glanced down at it. It did seem a bit less swollen than yesterday, though it was turning a lovely purple shade. "Still attached."

"Always good to hear," he said, his thumb grazing idly along my hip. Just that small motion was enough to make my breath catch in my throat and start a pulsing low in my sex.

I reached down and brushed my thumb over his lower lip. He bit down on it and I inhaled sharply at the look he sent my way. We might have been closer to the end of the game now that we were with everyone else, but I knew he was thinking what I was—that we wouldn't have minded a few more days alone in our small cove by ourselves.

"Hey," someone called nearby, and it came with the sound of someone approaching through the sand. "You guys awake?"

Heather, from Team Five. I pulled away from Dean and shot her a guilty look. Her hair was pulled into two pigtails on either side of her face and she gave us both a curious look that had me blushing.

"Am I…interrupting?" she began.

"Nope, we were just waking up," I said. "Breakfast ready?" I began to slide off of the bed platform, then frowned down at my ankle. Drat. Still stranded.

"Here, I'll help ya," Leon said to my side, and before I could protest, he was swinging me up in his arms and carrying me over to the fire with the others. Alarmed, I shot a look over at Dean, who looked less-than-thrilled with Leon's actions. His fist was clenched—angry?—and I watched him calmly lower it and delivered a cheerful smile to Heather, reaching over to tweak one of her pigtails in a flirty manner.

I didn't like that at all, especially when she giggled and poked him back. "Tribal Summons this morning."

"Already?" I asked, but my question went unanswered as Leon set me down on one of the log-seats in the middle of camp. All eyes turned to my ankle.

"It's better today," I assured them, despite my grand entrance. All that focus on my injury made me nervous. But then Lana came and sat next to me, linking her arm through mine, and the nervous feeling fell away. She was doing her best to show everyone that things were fine, and she was supporting me. I appreciated it, too.

"We already read the mail once. Sorry we didn't wait for you," she said in a tone that wasn't that apologetic after all.

"No worries," Dean said in his cheerful drawl. I took a cue from his manner and didn't protest, though part of me didn't care for it. Being on an entire tribe of people was different than just hanging out with one. "Can we see it?"

Shanna handed Dean the card, and he immediately handed it to me before he even had a chance to read it. I flushed at that casual gesture that seemed so completely uneasy to me, and my face turned bright red. I flipped over the note and gave (what I hoped was) a casual laugh. "He knows I'm impatient."

No one else laughed. Awkward.

With that, I began to read aloud. "Roses are red, violets are blue, keep your team in the lead, don't be number two. The sky is blue, the grass is green, there can be only one winner from the chosen team." I flipped the card over to make sure that I wasn't missing anything. Nada. "That's, uh, interesting."

"Any thoughts?" Alys asked me.

"They need to hire better writers for this show," I said. "They rhymed "team" with "green.""

"She meant the challenge, you egghead," Lana said and pinched my arm, a little hard.

"Ow! And I know she meant the challenge," I said, trying not to sulk. Great, now my arm throbbed in addition to my ankle. "Obviously they're going to split us into teams, right? And I guess whichever team advances, only one person gets to win?"

"That's kind of what we thought too," someone else admitted.

The conversation spiraled out from there, and soon everyone forgot about the awkwardness between Dean and I, and Heather seemed nonchalant. Only Lana watched me with hawk-like eyes as the team discussed if teams would be picked or randomly chosen.

"What if it's a running challenge?" Someone said, and immediately all eyes swung back to me.

I forced myself to smile in a lighthearted manner. "Then I guess if it is, I won't be much of competition, will I?"

Several smiled at that. Dean didn't, but he didn't frown, either. Instead, he took the note from my hands and read it thoughtfully again, saying nothing.

I had no idea what was going on in his mind.

LUCK MUST HAVE BEEN SMILING ON ME, BECAUSE WHEN WE GOT TO THE challenge, I saw chairs instead of an obstacle course. That was a good sign.

"You'll be divided into two teams for this challenge," Chip said, as if we hadn't already guessed as much. "The first round will be trivia—how much do you know about this show?" He paused to let that sink in, and then continued. "The next round will be for the winning team alone—you will compete individually in an endurance challenge."

My heart fell at that. So much for hoping my ankle would not be a liability.

Team captains were randomly selected—Lana was one, and to my surprise, Dean was the second one. Lana had first choice, and she selected Riley, the strongest remaining guy. No surprise there.

"Dean, select a female player," Chip reminded him.

"I pick Abby," he said, and glanced over at me.

"Interesting choice," Chip said. "Care to explain it?"

"Abby's smart," Dean said with a shrug. "And we work well together."

I hobbled over to his side and looked out at the remaining players. It could be seen as a strategic move, really—I was too hurt to compete in the second half of the competition. Providing our team got past the first round, it'd be a smart move and I wondered if the others saw it that way.

Didn't seem like it. As I glanced over at Heather, she made a kissy face and giggled, which caused me to flush. So much for strategy.

The rest of the teams were picked accordingly. Leon ended up with Lana, and we had Will, Alys, and Heather in addition to myself and Dean. After teams were selected, we moved to the designated playing area. Two benches had been left—one for each team, with a slate for each team to write their answer. I sat on the end of our bench as Dean took up the chalk opposite Lana, who stood at the chalkboard for her team.

"First team to get ten points for correct answers will move on to the next round," Chip said. "First question…"

The trivia questions were random things about the islands—the history of the native people of the Islands, the explorers that found them, and a few questions scattered here and there about the game and players that had been voted off. It was clear from the get-go that Lana's team was lacking in the history department. As for me, since my day-job was to retain useless bits of trivia and pepper them into magazine articles and book reviews, well, we did really well. By the time Dean put down the chalk and our team hit ten points, I'd been responsible for half of them. My shoulders ached from so many vigorous slaps on the back. We were winning, and it was exciting.

"Let's move on to round two," Chip said, and everyone stood but me. "The endurance part of the challenge." He gestured to the nearby edge of the water. "Do you see the poles out there in the distance?"

Five poles jutted from the water a good deal out from shore. Each one was colored a separate color, and I had to raise my hand to my eyes and squint to make them out. More like a sprint than endurance, but it didn't matter because I wouldn't be able to do either.

"Your job is to run out, swim across and get to the top of your pole. At the top of your pole is a lever you can release. Doing so will shoot your flag into the air. The person that releases their flag first wins immunity and will be safe at our first Judgment."

The others lined up at the designated starting line. Chip glanced over at me at my spot on the bench. "Going to participate, Abby?"

I could practically hear the smirk in his voice. Bastard. He liked seeing me suffer. "I'm going to sit this one out, unfortunately. Sorry." I was tempted to hold my injured foot out and wiggle it, but drawing more attention to it than I already had would be a bad idea.

"Contestants ready?"

"Set…"

"Go!"

I held my breath as Dean surged forward, his muscles flexing and golden in the sunlight. He was beautiful and lean and strong, and the others stood no chance against him. Within moments, Dean had cut through the water and swam twice as fast as his closest competition. His flag shot into the air a moment later, and Dean punctuated this with a yell of enthusiasm and pumping his fist. From my spot on the bench, I clapped excitedly, exhilarated at his win.

The others looked markedly less enthusiastic. I couldn't blame them—Dean was making the rest of us look like amateurs.

* * *

"So who are we voting for tonight?" I limped toward the Judgment campfire, a few steps behind Lana. Camp had been noisy, with everyone congratulating Dean on his win and chattering about Judgment that night. I'd thought the tribe would be pensive after realizing we'd have to get rid of someone, but they seemed buoyant. Everyone hung around camp and talked and laughed, and Dean was the center of attention. Shanna seemed to be paying a lot of attention to him as well, and that irritated me but I said nothing. After all, Dean was sleeping with me. We had plans for a Final 2 and who knew where it would go from there?

I didn't have a chance to talk to Dean, either—people were constantly around and I was avoiding walking because of my ankle. I had waited all day to try and get a few moments alone with him, but the only time he'd left camp was to go get water with Lana. When they came back, she'd given me a thumbs-up that made me feel better. Even if I hadn't had a chance to talk to Dean, she had my back.

Still, I was going in to the vote with no clue who to vote for. And when we lined up, Dean was at the front of the line because he had immunity. I pulled up the rear because I couldn't walk fast, thanks to my bad ankle. Lana loitered at the back near me, and I slowed down, pretending to catch my breath.

"So who are we voting for?" I leaned heavily on my makeshift crutch and put my other hand to my ribs, pretending to catch my breath.

She paused as well, waiting for me. Her hands were on her hips, and she flicked a glance back to the front of the line. "Riley. He's strong and we need to get rid of him."

Made sense. I gave her a thumbs up and we began to catch up with the others.

"I'll read the first vote," Chip said at the front of the room. He held up the first slate and I glanced at it with mild interest, more interested in Dean as he sat there with the immunity belt around his waist. He hadn't come over to talk to me today, and I wondered if his feelings were changing now that we were around the others? Maybe he wasn't interested in me anymore.

Of course, that was silly, I told myself as he glanced down at me and winked. One day wasn't enough to change a guy's mind about a girl....was it?

"First vote—Abby."

I didn't recognize the handwriting, but I wasn't surprised. If we had more immunity challenges that involved teaming up, I'd be a liability. Someone was bound to write my name down, but my Alliance had my back.

The next vote was my own handwriting. "Riley," Chip said, holding up the slate for all of us to see.

The next: "Will." That was random. I idly wondered who had bothered to vote for Will. He was a sweet guy and not exactly kicking anyone's butt in challenges.

Lost in my musing, I almost missed the next vote. "Abby."

I frowned, sitting up a little straighter.

Chip turned around the next slate with great relish. "Abby." And the next. "Abby."

Four for me. My pulse was pounding in my veins so loud that I could barely hear Chip over the roaring in my ears. "Fifth vote—Abby. That's enough. You have been exiled off of Endurance Island."

I sat in my seat, numb, before instinct kicked in and I got to my feet, leaning on my crutch. Hands patted me on the back and murmured that they were sad to see me go.

Big fat liars.

I moved forward to the Exile Archway and glanced back at Dean. Poor guy—I wondered what he was thinking at the moment. Was he upset? Angry?

But when I glanced back, Dean wasn't looking at me. His head was bent close to Lana's, and they were both whispering furiously.

A cold pit settled in my stomach. What was going on?

"Time to go, Abby," Chip said impatiently and put a hand to the small of my back. "You've been exiled."

"I'm going, I'm going," I hobbled my way through the archway and down the wooden steps. In the background, I could hear the others leaving the council area, and I felt a pang of loss as I stared at the empty darkness ahead of me.

What had just happened?

"There you are," cried one of the production assistants, and she rushed forward on the sandy path to help me walk forward. "You ready to go?"

"Where are we going?" I stared at her dumbly—she was so clean and fresh. I , well, wasn't.

"To the Exile camp. You're the first person in our jury and we've got special plans for you."

"Yay, me," I said warily, but allowed her to lead the way. Sure enough, she led me out to a dock and we boarded a small boat that took us to a nearby island. I could see the lights and the windows of a lit cabin in the distance. I should have been excited to see it, because I knew what was coming up—a real bed that I didn't have to share. A shower. Clean clothing. No bugs eating me alive. All the food I could possibly want to eat.

But I was still numb about what had just happened at Judgment. I couldn't get past it, not yet. It was like a raw wound. I wasn't hurt, but I was close. "So what happened back there?"

The assistant looked over at me, her brow wrinkling. "Back at the council? We won't know until someone reviews the voting booth tapes for the show." She shrugged. "Even so, seemed pretty obvious to me that you'd been set up."

It seemed pretty obvious to me, too. But I wanted to know who had done it. Who had flipped the entire tribe against me so completely? And what role did Dean play in all of this? Had he voted with them, or had he been just as surprised as I was?

I wanted to trust him, to believe in him, but my mind kept focusing on that last day in camp. Of Shanna with her hands on his shoulders and Dean laughing. Dean winning immunity. Dean unable to spend a moment alone with me after the challenge. Dean with his head bent toward Lana's after my vote, whispering madly.

It all left a sick feeling in my gut.

Eventually the production assistant—Jamie, I later found out—had me settled in to the cabin. There were a bunch of bunk beds and multiple rooms in the beautiful four bedroom villa, with a wet bar and the biggest, most well-stocked kitchen I'd ever seen. There were even a few people on hand to cook for me and fuss over my skinny, bug-bitten body.

After a midnight meal in which I'd eaten a little bit of everything they'd tossed at me, I found myself alone in the villa. Jamie promised to show me the impromptu studio where the crew was set up, but in the morning. And then there were post interviews and all kinds of promotional things to go through for the next few days, before the next person was voted off. But for tonight, it was just me, my chosen bed, and the shower I was dying to take.

The shower itself struck me as a palpable thing. Just like the cabin Dean and I had shared for a reward, this one had swinging wooden doors and a massive shower room. The reminder hit me hard, and I began to cry quietly before I'd even turned the nozzle on, and I let myself weep as I showered, soaped my body up, rinsed, and started the process all over again.

Stupid to get so worked up over a game. Stupid to cry about it. Stupid to think I wasn't going to get voted off. Strangely enough, those weren't the parts that bothered me. My restless mind kept circling back to Dean.

I'd fallen for the guy—hard.

And I was beginning to think he'd betrayed me.

Chapter Twelve

What the fuck just happened? —Dean Woodall, Day 22

A BUNCH OF HOOTING AND WHISTLING HERALDED MY ARRIVAL WHEN Jamie led me to the production crew. I gave her a puzzled look.

"You're really popular around here. Everyone loves you, especially the producers."

I blinked. "What? Why?" The looks they were giving me weren't cheerful as much as they were…well, a bit too personal. I'd chosen to wear a new sarong for a skirt and my bikini top, and I was regretting that decision. I should have sprung for something a little more sedate…but after a month on the island, this felt dressy to me, and almost too warm. My ankle was bound tight, and I wore a pair of slip-on sandals. My hair was in a pony-tail and I wore no makeup. Nothing to write home about.

"You and Dean," she said gently. At my continued blank look, she went on. "You guys, uh, well…your romance was on camera. The producers like that sort of thing. Good ratings."

I glanced at the camera men, who were laughing and nudging each other as we passed. "Romance on camera?" Something wasn't adding up. A moment passed before I began to get an uneasy feeling. "You mean…"

"Reeeeally on camera," Jamie confirmed. "We sort of have shots of you two everywhere."

I groaned and hid my face. "Oh my god. Oh my god. Tell me that you don't have us having sex on camera."

"Cheer up," she said, patting me on the shoulder. "At least we're not a cable network."

I groaned even louder. This whole experience had just gone from bad to worse. "Shoot me, please."

"Don't worry. The network has a no-nudity clause. Anything we shot that isn't family flavored won't be shown."

Somehow that didn't help me much right now, as the crew was giving me rather knowing looks. My face was bright red and I had a feeling it would be for a while.

"There's our first jury member," a voice said behind me, entirely too cheerful for my tastes.

I turned and faced a familiar man, dressed like he was out on safari and not on an island. "Mr. Matlock," I greeted, remembering the producer from our brief meeting in my boss's office. "How are you?"

"Sad to see you," he said, and clapped me on the shoulder with a big, callused hand. "Had no idea you'd turn out to be such an entertaining contestant, Miss Abby."

I blushed, shocked beyond words that he'd bring that up to my face. "Um…"

"The production crew are huge fans of that scene when you threw paint in Dean's face," Jamie interrupted smoothly.

I relaxed a little, though the blush remained on my face. "Oh. Wow, that feels like so long ago."

"Three weeks," Mr. Matlock agreed, and tucked my hand into his arm. "It's kind of a good thing that you're our first juror. This will give us plenty of time to go over the articles that Media Week should run about the show, and you can spend the rest of the time getting interviews and reviewing tapes."

"Great," I echoed, faking enthusiasm. Crap. I'd totally forgotten about the book. How on earth was I going to write about the time I'd spent here and avoid the topic of my relationship with Dean? It didn't seem right to write about it. That would just make everything…weird.

Er, weirder.

"That's wonderful. Let me know when you're ready to start on the tapes and I'll show you the area we've set up for your viewing room."

I glanced around the room. More of the smirking crew lingered, and I had a sneaking suspicion that they were waiting for Mr. Matlock to leave so they could embarrass the crap out of me. "You know, there's no sense in waiting," I said, keeping my voice cheerful. "No time like the present to start."

Anything to get away, pronto.

To my relief, Mr. Matlock was more than willing to show me the screening room. A few metal folding chairs were set in a small, tiled room and I was allowed to view reel after reel of TV footage. After showing me all the different gadgetry that the show had been able to afford (of which I appropriately oohed and ahhed over), I was allowed my choice of reels to watch, with minimal supervision. A guy was also in the room, but he was editing and had headphones on, and barely glanced at me.

I selected one file listed as "Pre-show interviews" and saw my own at the top of the stack. Ugh. I didn't want to see what I looked like on camera. I opted for the next one down—Alys. Her reel was rather short, but funny. It was odd to see her with ruddy, full cheeks and a face full of makeup. She also seemed to be rather high spirited going into the game, which was surprising. My memories of Alys and her grimly determined face didn't match the reel. I wondered how many other people didn't seem to match their 'game' personality. After watching and making myself a few notes on a pad of paper, I reached for the next one and the breath sucked out of me. Dean's reel. Overcome with a mix of emotions—shyness, uncertainty, dread—I couldn't seem to stop myself from placing the reel in and hitting "Play."

It was Dean, in a casual Nike T-shirt and a pair of jean shorts. His hair was ruthlessly short—a skull trim. The deep golden tan was still there, and I wondered idly what he did in real life. And that's when I noticed the looping red and blue ribbons around his neck, especially when he gestured to them.

"You want to know about these?" he was telling the camera, and laughed with delight, as if that were the funniest question ever. "Don't you guys know who I am? Dean Woodall, two gold and one silver in the last Olympics. Swimming. Yup. Yup, that's me. Money? I'm here for the challenge of the game." He hefted one medal and held it next to his cheek, grinning and hamming it up for the camera.

That pose seemed really familiar to me. So familiar that my gut clenched. Where had I seen that before?

The interviewer was laughing. "That your SI pose?"

"Cover shot," he agreed with the interviewer, and let the medal fall back on his chest.

Oh god. Oh god. Oh god.

"Tell me about strategy, Dean. What's your plan for the game itself?"

He gave an easy, lightweight shrug of those muscled, sleek shoulders, and my heart clenched at the familiar movement. "I'm looking forward to the competition. Test myself against elements…and the other players. Romance the ladies? If I need to. Anything to win, but I'm not specifically looking to meet a girl.

Romance the ladies? If I need to.

Anything to win.

Oh god. I was going to throw up.

This couldn't be real. No way. I turned away from the footage as Dean continued to go into detail about how he planned on flirting with the girls to get ahead in the game. His casual laugh grated on my nerves, and I couldn't take any more. My fingers fumbled for the pause button and I froze the screen. It highlighted on Dean's face and his sleepy, laughing eyes. He looked sexy as hell.

I wanted to punch him in the face.

TWO HOURS AND A DOZEN OF DEAN'S INTERVIEWS LATER, MY HEART had been shattered into a thousand pieces. The guy I'd slept with—the guy I'd gone crazy over—had used me. Every promotional interview was either about his past—as a playboy Olympic Medalist, or how he was going to be a major flirt in the game to use women to his own advantage, and when he didn't see the advantage? He'd discard them.

And while I initially didn't want to believe it, his words rang true over and over again.

"It's my goal to hook up with a girl partner," he told the camera with a laughing grin. "Preferably someone cute, but that doesn't matter. I need her to trust me, and when I've got her wrapped around my finger, I'm golden. And then when she's no longer any use to me?" He drew a finger across his neck in a classic gesture. "Done. Finito. It's all about me in this game…but of course, the girls don't have to know that."

I was such a fool. I thought of the joke I'd made about a grown man being unable to look masculine in a Speedo. He'd given me such a puzzled look at the time. I'd had no idea why. Now I knew, I thought as I stared at the Sports Illustrated photos of him in a Speedo and his medals. My heart sank.

DEPRESSED AND UNHAPPY, I SPENT THE NEXT TWO DAYS WITH A CARTON of ice cream in my hands and making notes in my journals. There was a ton of work for me to do now that I was off the show—completing interviews, taping media junkets, answering questions, and taking notes on how the crew worked around the set. Since I'd be writing a 'secret' expose, I got behind the scenes information on just about everything—from how they came up with the challenges to how much influence the producer actually had. It was rather eye-opening.

Two days later, the next Judgment was held. Since I had been voted off, I wasn't allowed to go back out to the Judgment Court, but watched via one of the feeds back at camp. Heather was the next one to be voted off— she wasn't surprised in the slightest, judging by her reaction. I watched the faces of my former alliance—Lana, Will, Leon, and even Dean—and they were expressionless as Heather hugged them and left. Everyone knew exactly why Heather was leaving. It wasn't that she wasn't good at the challenges, or annoying around camp. She was simply in the wrong alliance.

At least she knew what was coming for her, I thought with disgust. My gaze rested on the Immunity necklace that Dean wore around his neck. He was winning this thing handily.

A few hours later, Heather showed up at the camp designated for the jury. I greeted her with a bottle of wine and a celebratory pizza. "Welcome to loser land," I said with a smile.

"Check your bitterness at the door?" She teased, setting down her one muddy pack with a weary thump.

"No, the bitterness sticks with you," I said, hating the hard edge that crept into my voice. "Come on. You look like you could use something to eat." I led her toward one of the tables, noticing just how very dirty her bikini was in comparison to my cheery white tank top and yellow sarong. "Sit down and you can fill me in about everything that happened at camp after I left."

"Oh, plenty," Heather said with a grin, reaching for a slice of pizza even before she sat down. She took a huge bite and chewed with an expression of bliss.

I tried to be patient as she ate, even though I was ridiculously curious about what had been going on back at camp. Had Dean been upset that I'd left? Or was he one of the ones that had voted me out?

Eventually, Heather swallowed and reached for another slice. "It's been crazy at camp," she admitted. "Lana's running the show. Everyone listens to what she says and if you're not in her special club, you're gone."

I tried to ignore the sting of that. I thought I'd been in Lana's club, after all. I'd given her the last of my peanut butter, and shared my secrets with her, and look where it had gotten me. "So Lana voted for me?" I asked.

"All of them did," Heather agreed. "Dean, Leon, Will, everyone. Lana tells them who to vote for and they do it."

I flinched. Dean too, eh? "So Dean is in the little club?"

"Oh yeah," Heather said around a mouthful. "Mr. Gold-Medals? Definitely in the club."

My eyes widened in surprise. "You knew he was an Olympian?"

"Hard not to," she said with a grin. "First time I saw him swim off the boat, I knew who he was. Plus, he's real easy on the eyes. You don't forget something like that."

Shame colored my face. Apparently some of us did. Maybe I'd have remembered him if he'd have written a book instead of posing on the front of a Wheaties box. "I had no idea."

"He's killing everyone in the challenges," Heather said, reaching for yet another slice. She was devouring the food and I couldn't blame her. Two days 'out' of the game and I still felt the urge to eat every ten minutes. "Dean's mopping up everything. He's lucky he's in good with Lana."

"Oh?" I said, trying to play it casual. "Are he and Lana tight?"

"Really tight now that you're gone," she said, and it felt like a dagger in my heart. "Every time anyone turns around, he's got his head near Lana's and they're whispering about something. Lana's the one in charge but I wonder how much Dean has his hand in. Probably a lot more than I realized."

Me too. "I wonder if he's sleeping with her too."

Heather choked on her pizza. "You slept with him?" Her mouth hung open and revealed a half-eaten bite of pizza. "Are you fucking kidding me? On TV?"

My face grew hot with embarrassment. "I thought everyone knew. You guys were teasing us about it back when we merged."

"Oh my god." Her eyes widened. "Dude, we thought he was just stringing you along for your vote. You looked totally lovesick over him and we were convinced…well…that it wasn't, you know…"

"Mutual?" I offered. The thought hurt me far more than it should have. I ignored the tears pricking behind my eyes and reached for a slice of pizza myself. "They're playing to win," I said in a light voice. "I guess I can't blame them."

But I totally could. And I did. Dean and Lana had been playing to win, and they'd used me. I wouldn't forget that.

Days passed, the game went on, and the loser lodge slowly filled with more people. One by one, the tribe whittled down to just the Alliance, and then Will showed up, equally shocked and hurt that he'd been betrayed by Lana. Leon and Shanna and Lana and Dean made up the final four in the game, each one growing more gaunt and dirty as the days passed.

I still thought Dean was beautiful. I hated him now, but I could still enjoy looking at him, I supposed. Each person that returned to the loser lodge filled in a different piece of the story, but all of their stories lined up—Lana was running the show, and Dean sat back and let her call the shots. Meanwhile, Dean continued to clean up in challenges. They were an unstoppable duo, and it seemed to be a foregone conclusion that they'd be the final two. No one was really surprised when Shanna showed up at the loser lodge, and Leon a few days later.

Thanks to my ever-increasing amount of duties from the crew, I didn't get a chance to spend a lot of time with the rest of the jury. For one, I didn't want to—I was still hideously embarrassed that I'd been suckered by Dean. It was just as well, because when they found out I was here thanks to *MediaWeek*, they'd given me a skeptical eye and their conversations turned to whispers—no one wanted to be a chapter in my book. I couldn't blame them. I really couldn't. So I kept busy with the crew, filming highlights and reviewing the reels they allowed me, even going on location to film a TV special on 'The Making of Endurance Island'. And if I felt a little lonely and left out…well, that was the price I paid.

Soon enough, it was time for the final tribal council. For this special episode, we'd get to dress up in our swankiest gear and sit in front of the

two remaining contestants and listen to them answer questions. Then we'd
vote for the winner in an elaborate ceremony.

After that…home. And a chance to return to my old life. I couldn't wait.
I would have been thrilled if I never saw another island ever again in my
life. Ever.

That didn't stop me from trying to look my best for the big finale,
though. All the voted–off women clustered in the single bathroom in the
lodge, applying makeup and fixing their hair (despite the overwhelming
humidity). I was no different; I wanted to look my absolute best when the
camera closed in on me. I wanted Dean to see how ridiculously hot I was,
how clean and healthy and attractive.

And I wanted him to regret using me, just a little.

Of course, I was a wallflower compared to the other women in the lodge.
They all cleaned up way better than I did, which was a bit depressing. I
wouldn't think about that too much, I thought to myself as Shanna strolled
past in a pale scarf-skirt that put my breezy island dress to shame.

Ah well.

When we were primped and ready, the jury filed into the show's van
and drove to the far side of the island, where the game was still being held.
A short drive later, the van parked and we spilled out, the jury members
laughing and a little bit tipsy. A frowning production assistant shushed us,
clipboard in hand. "When we motion for you, we need you to file in to
the council room in the order that you were voted out. Abby, that means
you're first."

I moved to the front of the line, my hands fluttering down my dress. At
the producer's signal, I straightened, tossed my clean, bouncy hair over my
shoulder and stalked onto the Council stage. It had been dressed up for
the final council. A bonfire burned in between us and the two remaining
contestants, and lit tiki torches dotted the oversized hut that we kept tribal
council in. Wooden masks covered the walls, and palm leaves had been
strewn about the set, adding an outdoorsy vibe to the interior, and soft
tribal music was piped in to set the mood.

I walked carefully forward in my swingy little green dress that brought
out my eyes and matched my only pair of heeled sandals on the island.
Moving from the darkness into the lights of the council stage blinded me
for a moment, and I concentrated on walking to the spot the producers
pointed me to. I moved there and sat down elegantly on the carved wooden

stool, then crossed my long legs, folded my hands, and stared at my enemies.

Lana and Dean looked filthy and exhausted. Lana's fragility was obvious, but there was a hidden core of strength to her and her posture was defiant. My gaze slid to Dean. He was more casual, leaning over one knee and resting his weight there. His cheeks were a little more hollow than I remembered, and his clothing was filthy, but he sat up straight as I walked in, and his eyes followed me. I ignored him, my back stiff with tightly-wound anger as the other jurors filed in. He tried to meet my eyes but I looked away.

Chip smiled at all of us as we sat. "Welcome to the final Judgment," he said in his best game-show voice. "It's been a long journey to get here—six weeks on the island. During that time, you've learned a little bit about each other, and you've competed together. You've fought hard to get where you are, but you've burned some bridges along the way. It's inevitable. And now it's their turn to judge you." He turned to the jury and gave us a brilliant smile, made all the more leering by the shadows. "Each of you will have the chance to interview the last two contestants, and when the interview is over, you'll cast your jury ballot. Vote for who you want to be the two million dollar winner." His eyes gleamed in the torchlight. "Understand?"

The jury nodded.

"Let's begin with..." Chip reached into a bag and pulled out a name written on a seashell. He flipped it over in his hand. "Leon. Stand up and ask your questions."

The big, tattooed man moved forward, and Lana turned to watch him. I took that moment to sneak a peek at Dean.

His gaze was still on me. Flustered, I broke eye contact and looked over to Leon, who was speaking. "Lana," Leon began. "Did you, or did you not, make an Alliance with all of us on this island?"

She gave a sly smile. "I did. I approached Will first, and then Dean and Abby since their camp was next to ours. Then when we had the switch, I suggested an alliance with you. And I had you pull in your old partner, and Will pulled in his. Then it was easy for me to approach the others and offer them the same thing—final four." She gave a small, unconcerned shrug. "You have to do some lying to get ahead in this game. It's unavoidable."

Leon turned toward Dean and gestured. "Is that true? Did you have to lie to get ahead in this game?"

"Yes," said Dean immediately.

My eyebrow went up.

"You want to elaborate?" Leon crossed his arms over his chest, a scowl on his face.

Dean shook his head. "Nope."

Leon glanced back at Chip, and then moved back to his seat.

"All right, we'll move to the next member of the jury." Chip pulled out another shell and examined it. "Abby, you're up next."

My heart gave a painful nervous thump. I stood, unclasping my sweaty hands, and moved to the center of the stage. One of the cameramen zoomed in on me and that made me suddenly nervous. Swallowing hard, I met the gaze of the two contestants sitting across the fire from me. Lana had a confident smile on her face, but I'd expected that from her. She knew how to work people. What I hadn't expected was the smile on Dean's face. His gaze was possessive as he regarded me, his eyes roaming over my figure, and he wore a smile like we shared a secret.

I wanted to punch it off of his face. I cleared my throat, kept my expression calm, and focused on the two. "I'll start with Dean," I said in a light, careful voice. "Dean, did you fuck me to make sure you'd have my vote?"

His smile was replaced by a frown, and then a scowl. "No, of course not."

I turned immediately to Lana. "My question for you—is he lying?"

She glanced over at Dean and a small, smug smile touched her mouth. "He told me he was stringing you along for your vote."

"Now wait a minute–" Dean began.

Chip interrupted. "I'm sorry, Dean, but you had your chance to speak. Abby, did you have any further questions?"

I felt ice cold as I stared at the two of them. My eyes narrowed at Dean and I scowled back. "No. No more questions. I found out what I needed to know."

I turned and went back to my seat.

The rest of the questions passed in a blur to me. I clasped my hands hard in my lap so I wouldn't cry or anything embarrassing like that. I focused so hard on keeping my icy composure that the council blurred for me. Lana answered all questions glibly, freely admitting to scheming her way to the top of the pile. Dean seemed less inclined to answer quite so easily—his responses were terse and sometimes angry. It reminded me of him when we'd first gotten to the island.

"Those are all the questions," Chip said. "Now it's time for the jury to vote who they want to win the prize. Abby, we'll start with you."

I stood and walked carefully to the voting booth. A stack of blank slates was there waiting, and I took one and laid it flat, then carefully wrote a name on the front.

The cameraman waiting there spoke to me. "Can you hold up your slate and explain to the audience why you voted the way you did?"

Very calmly, I held up the slate and revealed the name.

Lana.

"I'm voting for you, Lana," I said, and I couldn't even be gleeful about it. I was just tired and hurt. "You have my vote because you admitted to lying, and you never tried to get in my pants to get what you wanted in this game. Dean, I did *not* vote for you." My voice threatened to wobble but I rushed past it, my words spilling over themselves in a hurry to get out while my voice was strong and I was composed. "I'm sure that ruins all your little plans for world domination, and I hope it does. I hope you slept with every woman on this island and I hope your dick falls off because of it. You are the worst kind of person to sleep with a woman just because you wanted her vote. I actually thought there was something bellow that shallow surface of yours, but it looks like I'm the biggest idiot on this island, right? No longer. Lana, I hope you enjoy your two million dollars."

And I dropped the slate into the voting box.

Chapter Thirteen

I can't wait for this to be over. Now maybe we can get back to being normal again. And I can't wait to talk to Abby. It's been a long three weeks without her. I miss her.
—*Dean Woodall, Last Day of the Game*

ONCE THE FINAL VOTE WAS CAST, THE PRODUCERS MOVED INTO action. The jury was separated and shuffled away, reminded of our non-disclosure agreements. We weren't allowed to discuss our votes, or anything on the show until the finale would air on national TV a few months in the future. Each of the cast members was assigned a media escort that would follow us like a dog until we boarded the plane and went on with our lives. I was fine with that—I just wanted to get home.

So I quietly packed my things and closed up my cabin, and followed my escort out to the gravel parking lot where all the show's vehicles were parked. One or two of the cast had already left, and more were getting ready to depart. I saw Chip chatting with one of the cameramen. A few of the others hung back, talking while their media escorts waited, analyzing every word of conversation with a frown on their faces. Waiting nearby was Lana, and she scowled at the sight of me.

I ignored her, climbing into the passenger side of the waiting jeep.

"Wait," a familiar voice yelled, and I cringed.

Dean rushed to the side of my jeep, trailed behind by his media escort. "Abby? I've been looking for you. We need to talk."

I examined my fingernails. "I really don't have anything to say to you, Dean."

"That's bullshit," he said, an angry tone entering his voice. "We need to talk about what happened at tribal council tonight, because I get the impression that you're mad at me—"

"No talking about the council," barked my media assistant. "You are contractually obligated."

I gave Dean a tight smile. "Sorry. You're out of luck."

"Then give me your phone number—"

I shook my head. "I don't want to talk to you. Understand?"

He gave me a shocked look, and it emphasized how hollow his cheeks were. He'd played the game for so much longer than I had—it wasn't fair. "Abby, what the fuck?"

"She's got all she needs for her little book," Lana called from across the way. Both of us turned toward her. She was looking over at me with a look that mixed irritation and disgust. "Or didn't you know that, Dean? She's writing a nasty little tell all. Your little bed partner here was a media plant."

He recoiled as if I was diseased. "You what?"

"That's right, Dean Woodall, mister Olympian," I said in a bitter, angry voice. "I'm writing a book for the show. And I work for *Mediaweek*. Don't you think I'll have lots and lots to write about?"

His jaw tightened with anger, and he glared at Lana, then back at me. "Don't do this, Abby."

I gave a hard, bitter laugh. "Don't what? Don't use you to further my own ambitions? Oh the irony." I gestured at our vehicle. "Now, if you don't mind, I'm going to be late for my flight back home."

Dean took a step or two backward, the hard glint still in his eyes, clenching his jaw. But he said nothing else as the jeep backed up and slowly drove away, leaving behind my time at Endurance Island.

The assistant glanced over at me and gave me a cheery smile. "Bet you'll be glad to get home, huh?"

"Thrilled," I said in a voice that didn't echo my enthusiasm. Tears threatened to escape, but I fought them back. I was done crying over Dean Woodall.

*   *   *

"I TOLD YOU ALREADY, I'D RATHER WATCH THE SHOW BY MYSELF," I SAID
to my friend for the tenth time that day, holding the phone against my ear
as I flopped down on my sofa. I curled my legs up under me. "No watching
party, no nothing. I just want to have some time to absorb what I watch
without anyone staring at me. You understand, don't you?"

Todd made disappointed noises into the phone. "I guess. But you'll let
me grill you over it tomorrow? I hardly ever get to see you anymore."

"Tomorrow over lunch," I promised. By that time I should have had the
chance to adjust to whatever horrors showed on the TV tonight. "I'll buy."

"All right," Todd said, mollified. He chattered on for a few more minutes,
discussing work and how things had changed around the office since I'd
left. "I still can't believe you turned down the book deal and the TV special,
Abby. Girl, are you crazy?"

"Oh, they gave that to Chip," I said, waving a hand in the air even though
he couldn't see it. "They hadn't paid me anything up front, so as long as I
agreed not to do any competing shows, it wasn't a problem."

After the taping, the producers had cornered me and tried to get additional details about my relationship with Dean for the show. They wanted
to use our 'romance' as a major storyline and harassed me for details.
All kinds of details. Very *personal* details. When I'd balked, they'd tried
to sweeten the deal with offering me the hosting duties for an exclusive
'making of' special for Endurance Island. I turned it down as well. My
heart still hurt.

Being on Endurance Island had completely broken my heart and it had
taken months to get over it. I still wasn't sure if I was over it.

I smiled into the phone. "I must be crazy to pass on all the big money
gigs, right? I just...I don't know. I didn't want to air my dirty laundry? It's
bad enough that everything is going to be on TV."

He laughed at that. "I can only imagine what I'm going to see on TV
tonight. You're being all sneaky and evasive, which means it's worse than I
thought."

He had no idea. The nervous flutter in my stomach that had been present
for the last week was going non-stop. "Listen, Todd, the show's about to
start so I'm going to let you go, all right?"

"Tomorrow! Details at lunch!" He said and hung up.

I curled up on the far end of the couch in my apartment, reaching for the

Pepto Bismol as the opening credits began to play with a blare of trumpets. They'd created a montage of all the players, flashing their cast photos back and forth as they zoomed in on wilderness shots.

My face flashed onto the screen, pale and round-cheeked compared to the other women. I wore a bright, sunny smile and my brown, coiling curls had been pulled into twin ponytails that rested on my shoulders. I wore the tankini that displayed my name in hot pink, and it was clean and bright. This must have been prior to us landing on the island. I didn't get a chance to dwell on how I looked, because Dean's photo moved onto the screen next. It was an action shot of him rising up out of the ocean, rivulets of sea water pouring down his tanned abdomen. He looked amazing.

Just seeing that depressed me. Why had I ever thought a guy like that would be interested in a girl like me? He was a freaking Olympian, for crying out loud. I should have seen it coming. My stomach gave an unhappy gurgle and I chugged more Pepto.

Then the show started, panning in over the crystal blue waters of the ocean, and I was hooked. I watched, fascinated, as Chip's voiceover explained the rules of the game. The camera zoomed in on the twenty contestants scrambling for goods on the surface of the boat, and then the mad rush to get to shore. It was breathtaking to watch, and I settled in for the ride.

A few minutes into the show, it was evident that I was going to get a lot of face-time, and I cringed at the thought. The camera kept zooming in on my scowl. I scowled at Chip. I scowled at the others. I scowled at Dean when he picked me for his partner. My face flushed with embarrassment every time the camera zoomed in on my angry body, hands on hips. Had I really been that upset to be there?

Dean seemed to think so. The camera cut to a confessional interview, and Dean scratched his head, looking perplexed. "Abby hates me. I'm not sure what I did to her, but she genuinely hates me. I think if she could hold me underwater and drown me, she would."

I chugged Pepto again. Where was Dean's scheming? Where was the part where he vowed to use me to get my vote?

Instead, it showed us sleeping separately that night. Dean had another confessional with the cameras, and he expressed his dissatisfaction with how we were reacting to each other. "I just want to win and do well at this game, but I don't know how to talk to Abby without her getting mad at me.

It's like we can't speak to each other without snarling." He gave the camera a rueful grin. "She's lucky that she's cute or I'd have asked for a different teammate already."

It was painful to watch as the camera showed us sniping at each other, showed us breaking down at the challenge, and the paint I threw on him. It showed our dejected faces at the first Judgment Day, and then our surprise when we weren't the first ones voted off.

The credits rolled, and I stared at the TV in shock.

Was that all just good editing? Or was Dean really not the monster I had thought he was?

WEEKS PASSED. I WATCHED EVERY EPISODE LIKE A STARVING WOMAN presented with water, fascinated and horrified at the same time. Once each episode was over, I hit the replay button on my Tivo and watched it all over again. The days between episodes went by agonizingly slowly, and I found myself stalking my fellow castaways online to see if anyone had shared tidbits about the game. Everyone was quiet, as online contact was forbidden until the finale of the show. I hadn't bothered to get anyone's numbers, so I felt isolated watching the game play out.

And as it played out, I realized I'd been wrong about a lot of things.

I cringed when they showed the peanut butter moment on camera—I hadn't even realized that the cameraman had been nearby, taping us. It immediately cut away to a confessional. Dean's face, angular and just a bit unshaven, filled my television, and I felt a shameful twinge. He was so handsome, and his mouth was doing that sideways quirk that I loved, as if he were laughing at himself.

"I have no idea why I licked the peanut butter off of her finger," he admitted to the camera. "One moment she's just standing there, taunting me, and the next, I've got her finger in my mouth and I'm licking her with my tongue and I'm getting turned on. And now I can't stop looking at the way her butt looks in those bikinis."

I blushed, but felt warm on the inside. At least it wasn't just me that felt that way. The attraction had been mutual.

Our back and forth bickering—and subsequent flirting—was a heavy theme of the first two months of episodes. Our cabin where we'd shared the sleepover reward had obviously been wired with cameras. Luckily, the network chose to show things tastefully, and I only cringed with shame a few times, thinking of what my parents would say when they saw the episode.

From there, it got worse. We were constantly all over each other, and the cameras played that up. There wasn't an episode that we weren't giggling and falling into each other's arms, or sharing a romantic moment. Every time there was a night shot, the camera zoomed in on our feet, tangled together and sticking out of our small shelter.

It was so obvious, and very painful to watch. We'd been so happy. At least, I had been.

And judging from his confessionals, Dean had been too.

One particular confessional shattered me. It was after we'd completed a challenge, and had returned to our beach and spent time just chatting and putting bug oil on each other. We'd played in the surf for a bit, then laid on the beach, my head propped on his shoulder. We'd looked blissfully content. Dean's voice came over the shot, narrating from one of his confessionals. "You know, I like Abby. I like Abby a lot. She's different than most of the girls I've ever met. I never thought I'd find someone so stubborn and determined...or that I'd like it. But I really like her. I like hearing her laugh. I like catching her when she trips, or the cute way she sneezes. I like waking up next to her. When we first got here, I thought I couldn't wait to get home. But...now I don't know. All I know is that I'd like to keep waking up next to her."

Tears brimmed out of my eyes and slid down my cheeks. They were beautiful words. But was it the truth?

I started to grow nervous, waiting for the episode that I knew was coming—the tribal merge and my big betrayal. On the day it arrived, I turned off the phone and stocked up on Pepto Bismol, and didn't leave my couch, just in case there might be a commercial that would show me Dean's face, or an instance of us laughing and hugging again.

I'd grown to crave seeing those moments. I wasn't sure if it made me a sad sack or just sad that it hadn't worked out.

The episode began, and I watched with my gaze glued to the screen, hardly daring to breathe. It played on, and I watched my ankle give out in the challenge, and Dean carrying me, stroking my hair and comforting me. It went by in a blur of tears at that point, and as I watched the tribal council, I was not surprised by the results.

Dean held his slate up to the camera. He'd voted for Heather.

Lana held her slate up to the camera. It said "Abby." She made a sad face at the camera, then smiled. "Sorry girl. I love you to death, but you and Dean are way too close, and I want that money for myself. If I break the two of you apart, I get control of the game again, and Dean's got no choice but to be with me until the end. No hard feelings."

The votes were read. Rather than close in on my face alone, the camera split-screened and showed my face on the right, Dean's on the left. I looked confused as the votes were read, but Dean's reaction was immediate. He was shocked, and then furious. As I watched, he bent and started questioning Lana immediately, while I wandered off the stage and out of the game.

He hadn't betrayed me. Lana had lied.

Chapter Fourteen

*I don't understand what happened…Abby won't even talk to
me. What happened that she's so upset about? I can't even get near
her without production crawling all over us, worried we're going to
share answers. I just want five minutes with her, to see if she's all
right. If we're all right. Ugh. Listen to me. I sound like a weepy girl.*
—Dean Woodall, Post Game Interview

"YOU'RE ON IN FIVE MINUTES," THE ASSISTANT PRODUCER BELLOWED,
stalking past with a clipboard in hand. "Everyone make sure you're
mic'd up and ready to go."

I shifted in my seat nervously, my stomach full of dread. In minutes, the
lights would be up. I sat on the front row of a double-rise of bleachers on
the stage, artfully designed with an island motif. Somewhere on the far end
of the stage sat Lana and Dean. Once the lights went up, I'd be facing them
directly across the stage. The producers had made sure of it.

What a nightmare.

I felt as if I'd been living in one for the past few months. Every week,
the TV continued to show me things that I didn't want to see. Dean's

silent fury with Lana as they returned from the tribal council where I'd been betrayed. Lana had hastily backtracked, but Dean's fury would not be contained. It took several days for him to calm down, though he'd hidden it from the other contestants. I thought of Heather's confident assurances that he'd been in cahoots with Lana because he was constantly with her. Dean's confessionals to the camera revealed the truth—he was only with her all the time because he didn't trust her. If she left, she might run off and scheme against him again. So Dean stuck to Lana's side, oblivious of the rumors about them that flew about.

One episode focused on Shanna's vote out. She'd tried to work her charms on Dean to stay on the island. I watched, chugging Pepto, as the model won an overnight reward at a hotel. She immediately invited Dean, which made the other two furious. I watched as she sat close to him at the dining table, and reached over and touched his knee. Her smile was inviting. Skinny from hunger and tanned a deep brown, Shanna was still beautiful. I expected him to take the bait. Instead, he laughingly brushed her hands off and went to bed alone. His confessional was all about me— how he missed me, and how he didn't want anyone but me.

I wasn't sure if that made me feel better or worse. A mixture of both.

Eventually it was time for the finale, held in LA. They flew me out and kept me sequestered in a hotel. The next morning, a professional stylist and wardrobe consultant dressed me up. For the finale, I wore a plain white cocktail dress with a high waist and a tall halter neckline that tied at the back of my neck and left my back bare. It was lovely and showed the light tan that I'd kept (and evened out) long after the show was over. My shoes were simple white stilettos, and my hair was long and loose, curls cascading around my shoulders, and my makeup accented the green of my eyes. I looked amazing.

I wanted to be anywhere else.

I was kept sequestered before the finale—to keep everyone's reactions for the camera genuine, the assistant explained. The stage was dark as the jury was led out to their seats in the bleachers, with instructions not to talk until the episode was over. Dean and Lana were nowhere to be seen yet. I rocked in my seat nervously, anxious for this to be over with.

The show began, and I watched with my stomach clenching in anxiety. It played on a large screen overhead, and the audience was silent, rapt as they watched.

Lana and Dean were the only two contestants left, and the scene closed in with them on the beach. A confessional shot of Lana ran, and she smiled cheerfully at the camera, looking tired and dirty. She rambled about how she missed home and her family and was ready to get back to the real world…after she got the money, of course, she said with a grin.

The camera then cut to Dean. He grinned easily at the camera, a growth of dark beard lining his now-angular chin. He looked just as exhausted as Lana, but smiled at the question. "Well, I'm not quite ready to leave the island. I sure am looking forward to seeing Abby again, though."

Tears pricked behind my eyes.

"I've missed having her here with me. I liked this game better when it was just the two of us. I felt like…well, like I could trust her, you know? I haven't felt like that since she left. Feels…" he hesitated, and then gave a half-smile to the camera. "Feels weird, I guess."

The camera man said something unintelligible.

To my surprise, Dean blushed. He shrugged his shoulders and averted his face. "I think it's a little too early to talk about love."

My heart plummeted to hear that.

Dean kept talking, though. "But I do know that I miss her, and I want to see her again. I want to spend time with her off of a beach and in real life, and see if there's something there, you know?" He shrugged. "I can't describe it. I just…it's…" He struggled for a minute, looking for the right words. Then, he snapped his fingers. "You know how the first few days on the island, all I talked about was coffee and chocolate? I wanted sweets. Craved sweets. Needed them badly because I couldn't have them. That's how I feel about Abby right now. I crave her."

I felt my cheeks heat in the darkness, followed by the unhappy gurgle of my stomach. I was going to die of happiness.

I was going to throw up.

The show went through a few more jungle shots. Lana and Dean on the beach, scrubbing skin to clean up for the final Judgment. Lana and Dean chatting as they ate the last of the food in the camp. Lana and Dean walking to the final Judgment.

The final Judgment began. Dean's smile at the sight of me dimmed as the camera zoomed in on my coldly furious glare. It continued to flick back and forth between the two of us, recording our reactions as the jury questioned the last two contestants. The clips were shown out of order—and I could guess why. They were saving the most dramatic bit for last.

Then it came—the moment I'd been dreading. I watched in numb horror as the me-on-camera scrawled a name on the slate and held it up to the camera. *"I'm voting for you, Lana. You have my vote because you admitted your lying, and you never tried to get in my pants to get what you wanted in this game. Dean, I did not vote for you. I'm sure that ruins all your little plans for world domination, and I hope it does. I hope you slept with every woman on this island and I hope your dick falls off because of it. You are the worst kind of person to sleep with a woman just because you wanted her vote. I actually thought there was something below that shallow surface of yours, but it looks like I'm the biggest idiot on this island, right? No longer. Lana, I hope you enjoy your two million dollars."*

My tirade sounded even worse than I remembered. Bitter and angry, it poured forth from the camera, my voice ringing from the rafters of the studio. I cringed as the jury behind me began to snicker. As the me-on-camera slammed the slate into the crate and stomped away, I buried my face in my hands in sheer embarrassment.

The theme music began to play and the lights went up. The audience began to cheer.

I didn't look up, still utterly humiliated. I'd ruined everything. I'd been nasty and hateful to him when he'd been simply happy to see me again.

I couldn't look over at him.

Chip's voice boomed in over the roar of the audience and music. "Welcome to the finale of Endurance Island! Here, we'll declare one of these two contestants the winner of two million dollars!"

The audience cheered.

"And now, the moment you've all been waiting for…let's read the final tally."

I kept my eyes carefully averted, staring down at the floor as Chip began to shuffle the slates.

"The first vote…is for Dean."

A cheer arose from the audience. My nerves gave a little flutter of hope. Maybe my vote wouldn't matter. I looked hopefully over at Chip, unwilling to glance over at Dean across the stage.

Chip held up another slate. "Lana."

One vote wouldn't matter, I told myself. One vote.

The next slate. "Lana."

"Dean."

I hadn't seen my handwriting come up yet, and a nervous, sickly flutter began in my stomach again. The room grew tense as Chip pulled the next slate and carefully turned it. "Lana."

"Dean."

A fine sweat broke out on my body as Chip pulled up the last slate and stared at it thoughtfully. The audience was completely silent. I'd stopped breathing, my pulse pounding hard in my throat as I waited for him to expose my vote. As if pulled by unseen forces, my gaze slid over to Dean and I caught my first glimpse of him since that last night on the island.

Paler than the deep island tan, Dean's hair was cut swimmer short once more. Given what I knew about him now, this did not surprise me. He looked terrific, though. His face was clean-shaven and he wore a crisp gray suit with a green shirt that had an open collar. He looked casual and at ease despite the fact that we were on stage in front of an audience and on national TV to boot. His careful smile was easy and devastating all at the same time.

He glanced over at me. Our eyes locked.

I cringed and looked away.

"The final vote...and our winner of Endurance Island..."

Panic set in. I couldn't breathe. The world wobbled in front of me, blackness creeping around my eyes.

I turned and watched Chip slowly turn around the last slate, displaying my angry scrawl of handwriting. My furious voice piped in over the loud-speakers.

"Lana, I hope you enjoy your two million dollars. "

The crowd erupted into cheers. Lana and Dean hugged, and Lana bounced up and down with sheer excitement. Everyone on the jury bleachers stood and began to hug each other as Chip began to chat into the camera, giving a bit of narration as the crowd went wild with excitement.

I stood up. The world weaved and my stomach was so upset I knew I was going to throw up. I couldn't stay on stage. I tore off my microphone and bolted. Like a chickenshit, I ran off, pushing through the mob of people to get backstage. Away from the lights that glared into my eyes, and away from proof of what I'd done.

I'd cost Dean two *million* dollars. Any hope of ever speaking to him again had just gone out the window.

Shuffling into a back hallway, I ignored the production assistants that swarmed the back stage and leaned against the cool brick of the studio wall. People rushed past me with microphones and cameras, cords running all over the place. But now that I was off stage, I could finally breathe.

To make matters worse, I began to cry. Tears brimmed over my eyes and began to pour down my face, and I swiped at them repeatedly. This was stupid. I was not going to cry. I was not going to cry. I was not going to feel humiliated and lonely and like I'd made the biggest mistake of my life because I'd listened to others. *I was not going to cry.*

And yet I couldn't stop the hiccupped sob that broke from my throat. Hugging my arms close to my chest, I huddled against the wall, miserable and trying to keep the tears under control. Maybe they wouldn't notice I was gone. Maybe they'd cut to a commercial break and give me a chance to recover so I wouldn't go out there with red eyes and hiccups. Maybe –

A warm hand touched my arm, brushing across the bare skin. "Hey, hey…don't cry."

To my horror, it was Dean. I stared up in surprise, brushing my hand across my cheeks again. He was even more devastatingly handsome up close, his eyes clear and bright, his skin with just a hint of tan, and that amazing sculpted jaw that never left my dreams. I longed to lean over and kiss him. Instead, that just made me cry harder.

He pulled me against him, cradling me against his chest. Warm arms wrapped around me and his hand stroked my hair as I wept. At that, I cried even harder. Dean holding me felt so good. I hadn't realized how much I'd missed him in the last few months, and how betrayed I'd felt when I found out that he was using me.

Except he hadn't been. That just made me cry even more.

"Hey," he said in a low whisper, stroking my curls. "Don't cry, Abby." He gave me a little pat on the back and teased, "I should be the one crying. I lost two million dollars just now."

I choked on my tears and looked up at him in surprise. "That's not funny!"

Dean grinned down at me, his fingers brushing my wet cheeks. "Got you to stop crying, didn't it?"

My face crumpled a little at his sexy, playful smile. "You probably hate me now. I said some really horrible things."

"You did say some horrible things," he agreed. When I glanced down again, he put his finger under my chin and lifted my face so I was looking at him again. "But you didn't know what was going on."

Some of the awful tension in my shoulders eased, and my tears were drying up at his calm, soothing voice. I didn't move out of his arms, however; I liked being there far too much. "What do you mean?" I said in a wobbly voice.

Dean's smile turned sheepish. "I have to admit that I didn't exactly tell the others what was going on between us. It seemed a little personal and then you got voted off and I was so mad I couldn't see straight. But I couldn't let them see that or they'd vote me off too."

"I remember…" I said softly. I'd seen it all on TV.

"After you left, I didn't understand why you were so upset at me. Heather pulled me aside and tried to shame me for sleeping with you to get your vote. That's when I started to figure out what they were telling you. I didn't realize that all of them had been filling your head with all these stories about me and how I was just using you to get ahead. I talked to everyone and they all told me the same thing—they thought I'd been sleeping with you to get your vote, and they were shocked when I told them I thought what we had was the real thing."

I blushed at that.

"And then they mentioned you were a studio plant and you were working on a TV special and a novel about the behind the scenes gossip…" He let his voice trail off, letting me fill in the rest.

"It's true," I admitted. "I worked for MediaWeek and that was how I got on the show. I never applied. I didn't want to be on the show until my boss made me. But when I got home, I didn't…I couldn't…" I gave a small shrug. "I couldn't talk about what happened on the island. It was kind of… for me. You know?"

"You should have said something," Dean told me.

"You should have told me you were an Olympic swimmer," I retorted.

"I should have told you a lot of things," he admitted, pulling me close again. His head moved in closer to mine and I could see the blue of his eyes. "I should have told you that what we had wasn't some sort of ploy on the island to get ahead, and that I really liked you. And that I wanted to spend more time with you when we got home. But when you left, I didn't have any way to get a hold of you."

This wasn't going how I had anticipated. I thought he'd be furious at me.

Never want to see me again. And here he was confessing that he'd made a mistake? Dean Woodall? The cockiest man on the island?

"Abby?"

"What?" I said weakly.

"Do you...still want to give this another shot?" His mouth curled in the self-deprecating half smile I adored. "I'd love to spend time with you outside of the game, on a real date."

"But...the two million?" I couldn't get past that. "I just...I cost you a fortune, Dean. How can you ever forgive me?"

He laughed at that. "Abby, I have multiple endorsement deals. I don't need the show's money. I have plenty of my own." Dean brushed his fingers over my cheek, as if he couldn't help himself and he had to touch me. His voice dropped a little. "Is that the only reason you won't date me?"

I reached up and placed my hands on the sides of his head, pulling his mouth down to mine. After a moment's hesitation, his hands grasped me tight against him and his mouth began to devour mine. Like that, all the months of uncertainty melted away, and there was nothing but the teasing lick of Dean's tongue against mine.

A deafening roar swelled around us.

We broke apart, and I stared up into the microphone hanging over our heads. The cameraman grinned at us from behind his equipment. Our happy little reunion had been filmed and we were on national TV. Figured.

Chip emerged from the crowd that had gathered, beaming at the two of us, still wrapped up in each other's arms. "Looks like you two had a happy ending," he sang out. "All's well that ends well, and it looks like everyone here tonight is a winner."

The crowd cheered. We could hear the roar, even backstage.

"Commercial break," an assistant yelled, and Chip immediately lost interest and wandered away. The camera-men departed and the gaffe swung the microphone away from us. To my surprise, the crowd departed, leaving only a smiling Jim Matlock behind.

He approached us with his hands wide open. "Before you two go back on stage and finish the finale, I just wanted to say thank you for making some entertaining TV this season." Jim beamed at both of us. "You made this season worth watching, and the ratings prove it."

Dean took my hand in his, as if unwilling to let go of me for a second, and it gave me a warm feeling. "Thanks, Jim, but I think both Abby and I would have preferred a less exciting season." He flashed a warm smile down at me.

I returned it, my heart brimming. "I wouldn't mind some quiet time at this point."

"Well now," Jim said, clasping his hands. "It's interesting that you say that, because I have a proposition for you two. How about the two of you hook up as a team for my show The World Race?"

Dean groaned at the same time I did.

"If you're not interested in that, how about a reality show–"

"No thank you," I said hastily, squeezing Dean's hand.

He pulled me away from Jim, shaking his head. "I want to spend the next six months with Abby…without a camera in our faces." Before the producer could come up with another argument, Dean steered me away from him, back toward the stage that we were contractually obligated to reenter.

"Is that true?" I said to him as we walked back out. "Do you want to spend the next six months with me?"

Dean grinned down at me and pulled me close, not caring that we were in view of the crowd and they had started to cheer again. "Six months is just the start of the game. If we work well as a team, I'd like for us to make it to the merge."

I tilted my head and looked up at him with a rueful smile. "I don't do so well at merges, remember?"

"You will with me at your side," Dean said, and leaned down and gave me a long, satisfying kiss.

The audience roared their approval.

SOMETIME AFTER MIDNIGHT, THE AFTER PARTIES WERE COMING TO AN end. As soon as we had a free moment, Dean grabbed me and hauled me out to a cab. "Are you staying at the Four Seasons?" He asked me, even as he began to nibble on my ear.

"Second floor," I breathed, my nails digging into his arms as his teeth grazed my sensitive earlobe. I liked that far too much. "You?"

"Fifth floor," he said. "Wanna stay with me tonight? I have a suite."

"Sounds good to me."

It really, really did.

We raced through the lobby and into the elevator, ignoring the few partiers that tried to get our attention. We were done with Endurance Island and now it was time for our own personal reunion.

As soon as the door shut, Dean's mouth was on mine, and my fingers were ripping apart the buttons of his shirt. He hastily shrugged off his jacket and began to work the dress ties at the back of my neck.

"God, you looked amazing tonight. I couldn't take my eyes off you," he said, between fervent kisses that he pressed to my bare shoulders. "I thought you were sexy on the island but you're totally blowing my mind in this dress."

"Then I should keep it on," I teased, pushing his shirt off of him and displaying the tanned, ripped chest that I'd dreamed about for the last six months. I gave a sigh of pleasure at the sight and skimmed my hands over his abs. "You're so beautiful. I can't imagine what you see in me."

"You should be asking what I ever saw in other girls," he said, sliding the dress down my front and exposing my bra. He unclasped the front hook, exposing my breasts and nuzzling the pink nipple of one. "Though I do have to say these are amazing."

I gave a moan of delight, my fingers clenching against his ultra-short hair. "So you like me just for my boobs? Typical man."

He looked up, his arms locked around my waist, surprised. "Is that what you think of me?"

As he straightened, I felt flustered. Had I messed this up already? "Well, no. I just–"

Dean's hands cupped my face. "Abby, I like you because I respect you. You're one of the strongest girls I've ever met, and the funniest. I started to fall for you the moment you pushed me aside and made the fire for us. That's when I realized you were someone different than usual."

My mind focused on one part of that sweet speech. "You're falling for me?"

He kissed me again, his mouth gentle against mine. "I am. It seems silly to think you're in love after three weeks but…"

I knew exactly what he meant. "But those three weeks felt like plenty of time," I replied, smiling. It was true. I knew more about Dean and what he was like than I had anyone else. I knew the frown he got on his face when he was unhappy, I knew his playful side. I knew how much he loved to be in the water, and how quickly he lost his temper at puzzles. I knew that he liked to put his hand on my belly when we slept, and that he liked to wake up early. I knew that he never wanted to eat another coconut in his life. Being only with each other for those three weeks had taught me that. And most of all, I knew that we were good together.

So I wrapped my arms around him again and gave him another long, exquisite kiss.

"What was that for?" He said.

I smiled at him and leaned in. "Time for the merger."

SIX MONTHS LATER, DEAN AND I WERE MARRIED ON THE BEACH IN THE Cook Islands. Wearing nothing but tans and sarongs and beaming smiles, we held hands at sunset and stood ankle deep in the surf as one of the locals married the two of us.

The network was not invited.

Want to play again?

Turn the page for an exciting peek at *Playing Games*, the second book in Jessica Clare's sexy Games series, available now in ebook and print...

Chapter One

Why do I want to be on the show? Because the label told me to be here? It's not like I begged them to slap my face on TV. I'd rather be sitting in the studio. —Liam Brogan, lead guitarist for Finding Threnody, Pre-Game Interview Footage

"STAND IN FRONT OF THE CAMERAS, SWEETHEART, AND TELL US YOUR name." The assistant's voice rang out in the casting booth.

Nervously, I stepped forward into the bright lights, clutching the covered pan in my hands. I resisted the urge to shield my eyes from the light that was glaring right into my face and settled for only squinting a bit. "Hi there. My name's Katy Short."

"Tell us how old you are, Katy, and what you do." The voice behind the lights sounded utterly bored.

"I'm twenty-three and I recently received a degree from culinary arts school. I started a business. A cupcake business."

"Cute. And why do you want to be on *Endurance Island*?"

"Funny story," I said with a grin, trying to make myself seem as cutely approachable as possible—not something I'm good at, since my nickname is usually 'Cranky Katy.' "I'm actually not here for myself. I'm here because

my brother, Brodie, really *really* wants to be on *Endurance Island*. And I'm
here to show him some support. We figured he'd have a better chance if we
both auditioned on his behalf." I gave the cameras my best cheerful smile
and uncovered the enormous pan I held. "And so I brought a few presents
so you wouldn't forget us, courtesy of Katy's Short Cakes."

At the unveiling of my pan, there were a few oohs and ahhs from the
crew, which pleased me. It was early and they were probably hungry, so I'd
banked on bringing some of my infamous 'Short Cakes.' I'd stayed up late
into the night crafting them so they'd be fresh and delicious, and I had to
admit that they looked delectable. Delicate yellow icing was piped atop
perfect Dutch chocolate cupcakes in an ice-cream swirl design, and each
one was drizzled with a gleaming chocolate ganache and topped with a
cherry. The cupcakes in the center were missing the cherry, and I'd crafted
marzipan letters, spelling out Brodie's name using the same font that
Endurance Island used for their logo.

It was all part of our plan to get my brother on *Endurance Island*. He
talked about nothing else, and I figured if my cakes could help him, it was
worth spending a Saturday morning down here at the casting call. Brodie
had dressed in yellow and dark brown to match the cakes, and I'd worn
a matching outfit—brown leggings under an oversized yellow t-shirt that
read 'Pick Brodie.' My blonde pigtails were decorated with cherries. We
were totally ready to sell Brodie to the casting directors.

I held out the pan. "I brought this since I figured you guys might be
hungry."

Someone in the crew immediately stepped forward and grabbed the pan,
and a half-dozen hands reached into it, plucking out cupcakes. I grinned
as a few exclamations of delight hit my ears, and a woman with a clipboard
stepped forward, cupcake in hand. She licked a bit of frosting from her
fingers, then set the cupcake down and picked up her pen.

"These are amazing. What did you say your name was?"

"Katy Short," I repeated cheerfully. "And I'm here for my brother,
Brodie—"

"What do you do for a living, Katy?"

I hid my frown. Jeez. Did they have the attention span of gnats or what?
I eyed the cupcake she'd set down, the marzipan "B" listing to the side.
Well, hopefully when they did callbacks, they wouldn't be looking for a
'Rodie' instead of a Brodie. "I'm an accountant."

Blank stares.

Yeah. They really hadn't been paying attention. Figured. "I'm kidding," I told them. "I run an internet business called Katy's Short Cakes. I create custom cupcakes and ship them all over the country." I automatically pulled out a business card and offered it to the closest person.

The woman plucked it from my hand and glanced at it, then added it to her clipboard. "You're adorable, Katy. And sassy. We like that. So why don't you tell us about yourself?"

"Well," I drawled. "I'm here with my brother, Brodie. I'm pretty sure he's twice as sassy as me."

As if realizing for the first time that I'd mentioned him, the woman looked up from the notes on her clipboard. "There's a brother?" A knowing gleam caught in her eye and she reached over and took a bite of cupcake. She then snapped her fingers and circled her hand in the air. "Someone go find the brother."

"There's a brother," I agreed. "You're eating his 'B'. I'm here for him."

"You don't want to be on TV, Katy?"

I shrugged. "I'm more interested in launching my business. It sounds like it'd be fun enough, though." A sinking feeling began to form in the pit of my stomach. If I got cast and Brodie didn't, he'd kill me.

"How athletic are you?"

"Um." I thought for a moment. "I can carry three dozen cupcakes without breaking a sweat?"

There were titters around the cupcake box.

The casting director smiled, icing in her teeth. I automatically licked my own, hoping she'd pick up the hint. "Do you have a passport, Katy?"

I thought for a moment, then nodded. "I do. Brodie does, too."

"That's perfect," the woman said, marking something down on her clipboard. She glanced up again and yelled. "Did someone find the brother yet?"

A long, uncomfortable moment passed and I fidgeted on the stool. No one was asking more questions, but the audition tape was still rolling. Maybe this was a good sign. The fact that they were hunting down Brodie meant that they liked him, right?

Sure enough, my brother appeared a few minutes later, his blond faux-hawk noticeable next to the bald assistant that pushed him forward to stand next to me. Brodie looked excited, and I quietly crossed my fingers.

The assistant maneuvered Brodie to stand next to me.

He immediately gave me a noogie, ripping at my blonde hair with his knuckles.

I screeched and wriggled out of his arms. "You jerk!"

"Katy," Brodie said in a warning tone, the smile still on his face. "I'm just playing around."

"Then you don't mind if I kick you in the nuts when I play around?" I grumped, touching my hair. Noogies were fine and dandy—well, at least less obnoxious—when we were at home but here? In front of cameras? I was going to kill him.

Luckily, everyone laughed. "You guys are cute," the clipboard-carrier said.

Brodie automatically threw an arm around my shoulders, grinning a mega-watt smile for the cameras and dragging me back against him. "I see you all met my little sis, Katy?"

"Matching outfits," someone whispered. "They look perfect. Casting still needs a brother and sister duo, remember?"

"I know," the woman with the clipboard said smugly. Then louder, "So Brodie, you're the older brother?"

"Yes, ma'am," he said in a cheerful voice. "Katy came with me this morning to show support. She knows how badly I want to be on *Endurance Island*. We're close. Very close."

I snorted.

While Brodie and I were the typical bickering siblings, it was true about *Endurance Island*. As soon as we'd heard casting was coming to town, Brodie hadn't been able to shut up about it. This was his chance, he'd told me over and over again. Lots of reality TV stars used the show to get their foot in the door in Hollywood, and if this led him to a career in modeling or TV, he was all for it. I had my own doubts, since most of the people in reality TV shows weren't exactly killing it in show-business, but Brodie wouldn't be dissuaded.

"And you guys are local?"

"Yes, ma'am. We're from Broken Arrow, Oklahoma."

"Ever travel much?"

Brodie glanced down at me. "We had a family trip to Cancun once. Katy got so sunburned she looked like a tomato."

"He's lying," I chimed in, poking him in the gut. "I wasn't that red. And he's also neglecting to tell you about how he spent a week in London last summer, but I guess that doesn't count as 'travel' since he never made it out of the pubs."

There were a few laughs, and Brodie's arm tightened around my shoulders to an almost painful degree. Automatically, I reached over and pinched his side, like I always did when he tried to be the bossy big brother.

"Katy doesn't really want to be on *Endurance Island*," he blurted. "She's just here for me."

I pinched him again, wishing he would shut up. Where was my brother's suaveness now that the cameras were rolling? He was coming across like a tool.

"We're sorry," Clipboard Woman said. "But we've already got a couple of blond Southerners for *Endurance Island*. Casting's full."

Disappointment swept through me. Poor Brodie. He'd be heartbroken. I felt all the tension leave the arm looped over my shoulder.

"But," the woman said. "We're looking for teams for *The World Races*, and the brother-sister duo we had selected fell through at the last minute. We're currently one team short."

"*The World Races?*" Brodie asked.

"Teams?" I squeaked.

"Yes," Clipboard Woman said with enthusiasm. "We'd like for you both to come to Hollywood for a second round of casting. If you make it on the show, you'll be gone for a few weeks as you travel from location to location. It's a bit of a different dynamic than with *Endurance Island*, but it gives you a chance to see the world. What do you think?"

"A few weeks?" I echoed, my mind racing. I had orders I was waiting to fill. There was a wedding—my biggest order yet—scheduled two weeks from today and I planned on spending every moment baking and then driving the cupcakes down to Dallas before icing them to ensure that they'd be perfect. I couldn't leave for several weeks.

Brodie obviously knew where my mind was going, because his arm tightened around my shoulder again. "I'm sure I could get the time off of work."

I bit back a sarcastic remark. Of course he could. Brodie was a waiter.

"If you make it on the show, you'll automatically be paid a salary of twenty thousand dollars per team. The winning couple wins a quarter of a million dollars."

My brain froze. Wait. We got *paid* to be on TV? Twenty thousand dollars—my share would be ten grand. Ten grand would let me buy a state of the art website and some key advertising. That would make up for the bank loan I hadn't been able to get to truly launch my business.

"Shall I mark you down as interested?" Clipboard asked. "We think the two of you would be perfect. You've both got that Southern charm, you look adorable in matching outfits, and we love the brother-sister angle."

"We're in," Brodie said automatically.

"Twenty thousand dollars?" I blurted, unable to help myself.

Clipboard chuckled. "That's right."

"Sounds good to me," I told her. "When do we go to Hollywood?"

"Next weekend, if you're free."

"Oh, we're free," Brodie told her, squeezing my shoulder so tight I was pretty sure I'd have bruises. "We're definitely free."

Chapter Two

Have to admit, I didn't see any serious competition in the other teams. Get to know them? No thanks. I'll let Tesla do that. She's the people person. I'm just the guitar. —Liam Brogan, Day 1 of The World Races

Six weeks later

M Y STOMACH WAS CHURNING.
 The sun was beating down overhead, my yellow shirt was blinding me, the backpack on my shoulders weighed a ton, and I was pretty sure I was going to throw up as one of the off-camera assistants pointed us toward the starting line.

"Here we go," Brodie said with excitement, shaking my arm. "This is it. Are you ready?"

"I'm going to barf if you keep shaking me," I muttered.

"You should have eaten something," Brodie said, not an ounce of sympathy in him. He put a hand to his eyes, shielding the sunlight, and watched for the other teams to arrive. "Think we're the fittest ones in the race?"

"Don't know, don't care," I told him. "We get paid the same if we come in second or dead last, except if we come in dead last, we get a three-week vacation in Acapulco." Apparently as you were kicked off of the race, you were sent to a private beach house in Acapulco so no spoilers would leak onto the internet. As soon as I'd heard that? My motivation to compete had pretty much disappeared. Money and the chance to lounge on the beach for weeks? Who wanted to sleep in airports when I could sleep in freaking Acapulco?

He shot me a nasty look, as if reading my thoughts. "Katy, you'd better race like you've never raced before, or so help me—"

I raised a hand. "I will. Just don't expect me to be excited right now, okay? The only thing I'm going to be racing for is some Pepto."

He was right, though; I should have eaten something that day. Of course, I hadn't counted on being quite so nervous.

We'd arrived for the casting call last night and had been sequestered in the hotel rooms given to us. No contact with the outside world for the next three weeks, according to our non-disclosure agreements. No cellphones, no email, nothing. I'd had to temporarily put my business on hiatus, and it rankled a bit, but I just thought of that twenty grand. I'd make it up to the customers I'd disappointed somehow.

As soon as we'd woken up that morning, we'd been dragged into a whirlwind of preparations for the show. A casting assistant had been assigned to us and had gone over our bags one more time, removing everything that might interfere with 'the experience.' No sunglasses. No hats unless approved first by the network. No clothing except the mandatory gear they'd given us. One backpack apiece. No food or drink, nothing that would set off airport security, and for me, no bright lipsticks. They'd even gone so far as to assign me a hairstyle—the two dorky pigtails I'd worn for the initial casting call. They wanted to create a 'look,' they'd told us. We were characters on a show, and characters needed a memorable look. It was in the contracts, and I'd had no choice but to comply. My look, unfortunately, seemed to be backwoods cowgirl.

That was probably my fault. Stupid pigtails at the audition.

Our clothing was not so bad. The show had an athletic sponsor, and so everything we wore was branded with the same logo, right down to my sports bra and panties. Each team was assigned several shirts with the name written across the back, and a color for their team. Brodie and I were yellow, and I had black leggings with a yellow racing stripe, a yellow t-shirt with KATY written in big letters across the back, a matching hoodie, and a puffy yellow jacket for colder climates.

Once we'd been patted down, we were dragged to pre-show interviews. The network itself took at least an hour's worth of interview footage with me, one with me and Brodie together, and then we'd been rushed around to a few different radio and TV press junkets for use in the future.

And then we were dashed into a sedan and drove to where we currently stood—a football stadium. Not just any stadium, but the Cowboys Stadium. Row after row of seating loomed over us as we walked out onto the field, cameramen circling us.

We stopped in the end zone, like we'd been instructed, and waited for the other teams to slowly trickle out. We were the first ones on the field, which would give us a prime opportunity to gawk at the other teams as they arrived. Nearby, cameramen tested their equipment while others filmed us for intro shots. In the distance, the host sat in a director's chair getting his makeup touched up.

I already wanted to collapse from nerves. Who knew that a game would be so stressful?

Brodie nudged my arm again. "Look. Here comes the first team."

I couldn't help but look, since Brodie was trying to drive his elbow into my upper arm. We'd marathon-watched the two previous seasons of *The World Races* to try and figure out the kinds of people they were going to cast as our opponents. Like casting had mentioned, they definitely had a type of character they liked to cast: newlyweds, guy best friends, girl best friends (which they wanted to hook up with the guy best friends, naturally), a dating couple, siblings, a child-parent relationship, a gay couple, a D-list celebrity couple of some kind, and then a 'comic relief' couple. Sometimes the comic relief was a pair of rednecks. Sometimes they were nerds. They always did terrible in the challenges, since they weren't picked for athleticism.

Sometimes the team dynamics overlapped. The comic relief could be siblings, and then that would leave room for another couple or another celebrity or something. I was told from a gushy assistant that the producers liked to mix things up a little, but they stuck to stereotypes overall. We were creating a 'story,' she reminded me.

Like I was going to be able to forget? Characters. Story. Everyone in casting mentioned it every five minutes.

"Girl besties," Brodie murmured at my side. "Or lesbians. They look pretty strong."

"Way to be a creep, Brodie. Now *you* sound like casting." But I admit, I tried to figure out their stereotype, too. They *did* look strong. I didn't recognize them, which meant they weren't the celebrities, so they had to be the female best friends team. One wore a shirt that said 'Summer' and the other said 'Polly.'

They stood at a marked spot a fair distance from us, and the next team came out.

"Here's someone else. They're obviously mother and son," Brodie told me, nudging me and staring at a couple walking in behind the two female athletes. 'Wendi' and 'Rick' were easy to pick out, I decided. Wendi had gray hair and a matronly figure, and Rick, well, Rick was a skinny kid with long hair in his face, big glasses, and skinny jeans. The entire effect was supposed to make him look trendy, but it just made him look incredibly awkward instead.

More teams flooded out of the entrance, pair by pair. We saw Hal and Stefan, dressed in flaming pink shirts, holding hands as they walked in. Cute. I liked them already. Then there was a pair of blondes with enormous hair and loud voices that talked with their hands—Steffi and Cristi. Myrna and Fred were the elderly couple, though they looked pretty fit despite the white hair. There were a pair of alpha males named Joel and Derron that went into a military stance as soon as they arrived, which made Brodie frown. My brother didn't like competition, and that pair looked like they'd be tough to beat.

I was relieved to see a man and a woman with matching mullets, cowboy boots, tight Wranglers, and kelly green team shirts. Kissy and Rusty. Thank god. The comic relief wasn't us.

"Hey, isn't that Dean Woodall?" Brodie leaned in to my ear. "The Olympian?"

I perked up. I'd seen him on TV before. "You think so?"

"Yeah. Not happy about that. They sure did cast a lot of athletic people this year."

"I think he's retired," I told Brodie. I remembered him from *Endurance Island* last year. I'd been addicted to the TV, fascinated by the romance that played out between him and a fellow contestant. Sure enough, Abby was at Dean's side, dressed in a purple shirt to match his. Her curly hair was pulled into a loose ponytail on top of her head and when they came into line, Dean's arm went around her waist. Double cute. They were clearly the newlyweds *and* the celebrities.

Or so I thought.

"Holy shit."

I tore my gaze away from Dean and Abby to glance at my brother, Brodie. "What now?"

"The celebrities," Brodie breathed, staring down the field. "Holy shit, they got *Finding Threnody*."

"Huh?" The name sounded vaguely familiar, but I was more of a country girl. I was short and couldn't see around Brodie, since he'd moved and was now standing directly in front of me and blocking my view. "Who's *Finding Threnody*? It's a band?"

"They're huge," he told me. "Don't you know the song 'Dark Stars?' 'Worm in the Apple?'"

Um, okay. "Doesn't sound like my kind of thing. I don't like rock." When he paced in front of me again, I pinched his arm. "Stand still, damn it. You're not a freaking window."

Brodie sighed and moved back a step, giving me my view. Of course, it wasn't an unobstructed view, because the camera crew was hovering around them as they sauntered down the field, toward the starting line. It was clear that they were designated to be stars of the show. That was fine with me. I studied them. Both were wearing black as their team color, and the woman had hair that was dyed black with bright red ends. Her nose was pierced and she had small tattoos along her neck and sleeving her arms. The man had lip piercings, eyebrow piercings, and his arms were just as heavily tatted as hers. The man frowned at the group, while the woman gave us all an arch smile.

Their t-shirts read LIAM and TESLA.

Of course. Total rock star names. I could feel myself giving a mental eye roll as the woman sauntered up to the starting line and stuck her hip out, revealing jeans covered in chains and zippers. Naturally. "I can tell you right now I'll be glad when they're gone," I told Brodie. I'd taken an instant dislike to the two rockers. Maybe it was their attitudes, or the way the cameras crawled all around them, but they didn't seem to have the fun sort of spirit that the others brought. Hell, even Dean and Abby—who I'd thought were the celebrities this round—had seemed genuinely excited to be here.

Those two? Just acted a bit like they were slumming it to be around the rest of us. Which got on my nerves. Contrary to what everyone thinks about country girls, I'm not the most friendly and open type. I may have my hair in pigtails and wear jean shorts, but that's as far as the stereotype goes. You've got to prove yourself to me before I like you. And right now? Liam and Tesla were on my 'do not like' list until proven otherwise.

I glanced around, but no one else was coming out of the stadium. I quietly counted teams as the cameras did another pan of us lined up on the starting line, scoping each other out. Ten teams. Ten men, ten women. I wouldn't be the fastest woman, I guessed, judging by the competition, but I wouldn't be the slowest, either, so that was fine with me. And Brodie was fit. Our odds were decent.

"*Makeup*! It's hot as piss out here and my forehead is shining. Where's the goddamn makeup artist?"

All eyes immediately turned in the direction of the angry voice. My jaw dropped a little as I saw Chip Brubaker, the normally smiling host of this show and *Endurance Island*. As I watched him stalk down the field, he grabbed a powder puff out of a woman's hand and dabbed at his forehead. "When I say makeup, you come running. Understand?" he yelled again.

I leaned in and told Brodie, "Guess his smiles are just for the camera." I saw Abby roll her eyes at the host's antics.

Chip finished patting down his face, examined it in the mirror held up for him, and then strode past the scurrying assistants. Someone pointed for him to stand on an X marked on the grass, and he did. As soon as he stepped there, it was like a light switch was flipped. His face lit up in a friendly smile and he grinned at us as if we were his new best friends. Cameramen immediately circled, filming.

"Welcome to *The World Races*! I'm your host, Chip Brubaker, and you're about to undertake an incredible journey around the globe." He spread his arms in a magnificent gesture. "You'll travel to exotic locations and foreign countries, competing against each other for a quarter of a million dollar prize."

We cheered and clapped appropriately at that. Brodie was getting excited. He bounced on his feet in place, which was just making me anxious. I clutched the straps of my heavy backpack and concentrated on Chip as he rattled off the rules of the game. Blah blah find a clue, perform a challenge to win a *World Games* disk. Each teammate had to compete to win an individual disk and then there was a team disk. Once you had all three disks, you could advance to the finish line for that round. It was the same as it was every year.

"This time on *The World Races*," Chip said, and then gave an ominous pause. "We're switching the rules up on you a bit. The team that conquers the first country on our map? Wins an Ace in the Hole." He held up a big, obviously fake looking Ace of Spades that was larger than a sheet of paper. "This ace will allow that team to save one other team at any point in the game."

"Why would we want to do that?" I hissed at Brodie under my breath. "I thought the object was to get rid of everyone else?"

He shrugged and gave me a 'shut up' look.

"You can use this ace to your advantage and save a team you're allied with," Chip said. "Or not. The choice is yours. There will only be two aces in the entire game."

The cameras suddenly swiveled again, startling me. All but one began to film our reactions as Chip raised his hand in the air.

"Are you ready to begin *The World Races*?" Chip bellowed. "At the far end of this stadium, you'll find that the opposite end zone is covered with hundreds of footballs. Ten of these footballs are numbered, and the number you get pertains to your airline seat. Only teams one, two and three will be on the first flight out. Good luck! May the best team win!"

Nervous butterflies began to sprout in my stomach.

Chip lowered his arm. "GO!"

We ran.

BRODIE WAS THE FIRST ONE AT THE MASSIVE FIELD OF FOOTBALLS, AND I wanted to cheer my brother on. I stumbled early, twisting my ankle, and yelped in surprise. I recovered quickly and limped over to the footballs, the last one to arrive. Ignoring the cameras that hovered like vultures, I stared at the others as they pushed forward. People were tossing their packs aside and grabbing footballs like they were covered in gold.

Okay, clearly I'd missed out on the memo that told us we had to act like insane people.

I picked my way forward and kicked aside a football, looking for a number.

"Hurry it up, Katy!" Brodie bellowed at me. "Flip them and flip them fast!"

I sighed and shrugged off my backpack, tossing it aside and then diving into the fray. People were shoving and pushing like wild animals. I charged into the fray, grabbing the first football and flipping it over. Nada. I tossed it back down to the ground and headed for the next. And when that one was blank, the next. And the next.

"I got six," someone called. Another team yelled out their number—nine—and were less excited. No one wanted a high number.

I grimly picked up football after football, looking for a number amidst the chaos. I'd probably flipped about twenty footballs and dodged the other pushy contestants (and rolling balls) when I noticed one sitting alone at the back of the field, clearly overlooked. I could see a hint of white behind the football stand and a clench in my stomach told me that this was a numbered ball. Perfect!

As soon as I began to run for it, the rocker guy did too. Frowning, I picked up the pace, running faster. He didn't slow down. That son of a bitch had seen it and was going to race me for it.

We both dove for it at the same time. I landed on the ball, triumph rolling through me.

He landed on top of me.

The air blew out of my lungs. I groaned, wheezing, even as the ball popped out from under me and launched into the air a foot.

It bounced once. The rocker rolled off of me and neatly plucked it from the ground.

I remained on the ground, struggling to breathe.

He moved to stand over me and offered a hand down, ball tucked under his arm.

I slapped it away, my chest burning with the need for air.

He looked down at me a moment longer, shrugged, then flipped the football in his hand. "I got number two," he called out. Somewhere in the distance, I heard his partner squeal with delight.

Damn it! That jerk had just stolen second place from me. I clutched my ribs and groaned, forcing myself to my feet. A camera hovered nearby, no doubt catching my black scowl as I staggered to the next football and began to flip.

The field was clearing out as teams departed. Brodie trotted up to me, a football in hand. "I can't believe he stole number two from you. You should have fought him."

I rubbed my ribs. "Thanks for asking, Brodie. I'm fine."

He raked a hand through his hair, clearly frustrated. "Sorry, Katy. You ok? Seriously? Want me to get a medic or something?"

"No. I just need to suck it up. My pride smarts more than anything." I nodded at the football under his arm. "What's that one?

"I found number ten," he told me, disgruntled. "Keep flipping and maybe we can find something better."

I rubbed my ribs one more time. "'Kay."

More teams departed around us, and after about five minutes, I looked up and realized that the team that had found the number nine was handing in their football to Chip Brubaker. That left just us on the field. We were stuck with number ten. Brodie straightened and tossed aside the football he'd just picked up, as if coming to the same conclusion.

The race had just started, and we were already last.

Playing Games is available now in ebook and print.

About the Author

JILL MYLES writes under three pen names - Jill Myles, Jessica Sims, and *USA Today* Bestseller Jessica Clare. As Jessica Clare, she writes erotic contemporary romances with a dash of fun.

For more about her upcoming releases or to sign up for her newsletter, go to www.jillmyles.com.

Made in United States
North Haven, CT
01 May 2024

51982687R00105